NINO'S SONG

A novel by

LEAH COBHAM

'I see your strength, my child, as the strength of the lioness, who roars louder than any other four-footed creature, or as the strength of the female eagle, who, rising to the heights of the atmosphere above the male, and perceiving the entire Earth before her as a small pearl, focusses on and sees her prey, cuts back her wings and swoops down upon it – so I see your life as led by the Holy Spirit.'

Sara – Nino's Tutor, Jerusalem, 3rd century BCE.

First published in Great Britain in 2015 by §
An indie publishing house.

For
Richard Charles Cobham

Contents

შენ ხარ ვენახი, ახლად აყვავებული,
ნორჩი კეთილი, ედემს შინა ნერგული,
და თავით თვისით მზე ხარ და გაბრწყინვებული.

You are a vineyard, newly blossomed.
Young, beautiful, growing in Eden,
You yourself are the sun, shining brilliantly.

1: Erekle Street

The house crumbles around us. Paint-flake motes drift within golden shafts of sunlight, guiding us as we pick our way through a rubble of memories and stories. It is August 1st 2014, and my friend Nino's childhood home on Erekle Street invites the three of us, Nino, Eliso and me, to cross the threshold into its past. We all have our different reasons for searching through the ruins, but I am looking for a particular picture of a saint. I am chasing her magic, and have been ever since my relationship with The Republic of Georgia began in 2009. I can feel she is close by.

My friend Nino, the ethnomusicologist, named for the saint I am seeking, stumbles. Her black headband is covered in dust. She leans wearily against the cold stone window frame, disorientated. As I watch, her fingers crawl along the cracked surface, seeking something under the frame. Her body stiffens as she traces her finger down along the pitted masonry which leads like some ancient pathway to a broken and jagged floor. Squatting, she prises a board free with her fingers and reaches into the darkness below. Eliso calls urgently from the other room. Nino's head jerks towards the sound, then back to me.

"She must not see this," she mutters, falling heavily to her knees, reaching further and deeper into the hole. There is a pause as her plump forehead wrinkles in concentration. Just as Eliso calls out again, Nino extracts a wooden box from the darkness and holds it up to me.

"In your bag. Put it in your bag." Her voice is low, urgent, absorbed by the dead spaces around us and, as she heaves herself to her feet, I move to steady her and slip the box into my rucksack. It feels heavy. Eliso's long shadow touches my foot. I spin round.

"Come," she commands. "Saint Nino is in here."

I glance at my friend, Nino, whose eyes smile in her grimy face. I offer her my hand and together we pick our way across decades of decay and neglect. On the far wall, next to a blackened and broken fireplace, I see an icon of Saint Nino. The frame is rotting in places, and a bruised age spot threatens to obscure her jewelled halo. I search for her eyes. I see a dark and knowing truth glowing with wisdom in the half-light of the derelict room. Finally, just two days before I leave Georgia, I have found her, and I am bewitched. We stand together, Nino, Eliso and I.

Nino takes a fine golden chain from around her neck. On it is a tiny golden key. "It's for you: it belonged to another Nino – my great aunt," she says, pressing it into my palm. Beads of perspiration gather on her top lip, and her soft flesh yields as I hug her in thanks. Eliso's eyes roll and I detect an all-but-inaudible *tut*. Eliso is not a sentimentalist. Nino is tired, the effort to return to this, her old family home in the old town of Tbilisi, has exhausted her.

"Why don't we go down to the old town and get a drink?" I suggest. Nino looks at me, looks at my bag, and finally looks up to the saint on the wall. She crosses herself and reaches for Eliso's arm. Nodding, she turns away and, as they head towards the glassless window frame we had clambered through earlier, she calls back to me. "Bring Saint Nino, she is for you also."

There is a heavy stillness in the room, now that I am alone. I take Saint Nino from her place on the wall. Scorch lines leave behind a ghostly imprint of her frame, and as I shroud her in my headscarf, I shiver, despite the heat of midsummer. I look around me, checking that Eliso has gone, and take the box from my bag. The grime that covers it is mixed with the charcoal that smudges my fingertips as they explore the swirls and bumps of the wood. The hinges, partly rusted, break in two as I lift the lid. Like a doll within a doll, a box nestles within this box. It is exquisite, made of ebony and ivory, and with a tiny golden lock. As I peer at the delicate craftwork, the sun shifts, and a shaft of light penetrates the broken roof and warms my skin. I hold the tiny golden key Nino gave me, and holding my breath, slide it into the lock. It turns effortlessly. My breath catches. The first thing I see is a golden locket, then a little golden turtle with emeralds for eyes, and then a golden nugget. A crumbling, dried and faded rose has stained the blue velvet interior, and as I blow the ashes of past memories aside, I see a book. I lift it gently. Beneath, there is a pair of cracked spectacles with round frames and twisted arms. I open the book. It is a diary. It is Nino's Song.

2 : Delayed due to a Suicide

Later that night, as Eliso potters in the kitchen, I sit on the balcony of her Tbilisi flat. The heat hangs in the air like thick velvet curtains, stifling. Once I hear the comforting sounds of cooking, I reach into my bag for the diary and open the fragile pages carefully. I squint and see that it is in careful schoolgirl English with a smattering of looping Georgian script here and there. My heart flutters as I leaf through the pages. I reach for my glasses and, in the dim light, press my nose to memories now lost in the faded dusty script.

***

May 26th 1918

Dear Diary,

ჩვენ ვართ დამოუკიდებელი! Chven vart damoukidebeli! We are Independent! At least that is what Grand-Papa says. He shouted it as he ran through the house early this morning, wound the gramophone up, and danced down the path to the bottom of the garden! Quite what the neighbours will say I don't know. Then he picked me up by my waist and spun me round and round. One of my ribbons fell out. 'We are Independent, we are Independent,' he called through the hallways and out of the windows and onto the street. He started to sing so loudly, I am sure they heard him all the way down to the river. I have never seen his eyes shine so brightly, not even when he became a professor at the university.

Mother was not happy, however, and kept weeping and crying out for Papa. But Grand-Papa did not care. She followed him around, flapping the dusting cloth and closing the curtains as he opened them. He quite forgot that the early morning sun stripped the furniture of its colour. 'What does it matter?' he said. He wanted light in the house. Light had come into the hearts and souls of the Georgian people, he said. We could all now be free. Keti and I skipped after him, sliding up and down the polished floor until Grand-Mama caught me by my ear and bustled me outside, telling me to calm down for fear of a headache. She sent Keti to the kitchen to get tea.

I tried to go back inside to hear about this Independence, but she kept waving me away and when she had had enough of me, she shut the door. Why did she do that? I will be 14 next birthday, and then we will all go to Europe to visit the great university where Grand-Papa says I will see such sights and wear such dresses. I want to visit the Conservatoire and hear Mozart played. Perhaps Grand-Papa's friend will consider me as a student when I am older.

I was dreaming, dear Diary, about studying and being a great professor when Haim, the Jewish boy from next door, started to beat the sheepskins and carpets hanging on their garden line. What a sound it made! It was too early for this daily ritual. I was sure he had just come out to see what all the commotion was. I sat on an upturned wine jar under the grape vines, next to Mother's herbs, to wait and see what would happen next. At least it was shady there, and cooler. Honestly, could these people not be quiet for one minute? My head was aching from all the not knowing and I knew if I started to grind my teeth and Mother came out and saw me, she would shout louder even than the cries of 'Damoukideblobis! Independence!' that rang out through Tbilisi's streets. It was at that moment, that first, delicious moment, that I saw something peeking out from under Mother's prized flower bed, just by the far wall. It was nothing more than a tiny golden speck .

And, dear Diary, I am holding it as I write and I must say it is heavy for something so small. I cannot let it go. It is quite content to sit, my glorious golden nugget, warm and cosy in my palm.

Good night.

Nino

***

Five months previously, I had been sitting at my kitchen table, in Wakefield, with Keti, Nino the ethnomusicologist's sister. Spring was around the corner and I was restless. An icon of Saint Nino watched as we chatted in front of the open fire. "Will I be safe if I return to Georgia?" I asked.

"My sister, Nino will travel with you," she said. "She will introduce you to women who are extraordinary, who are inspiring, who will share their songs with you." Named not only after the saint, but also after her great aunt and various other women in her lineage, Nino read ethnomusicology at Tbilisi University. She was travelling through Georgia in the summer, researching her latest paper. I was already captivated by the music of Georgia, and fascinated by how often the pagan goddess, Nana, whose name had morphed into Nino, appeared in pre- and post-Christian folk and ritual healing songs. Saint Nino's golden cross glinted in the firelight. I was filled with indecision. I wanted to find her, but did I have the courage to go and search for her?

The last time I was in Tbilisi, during February 2012, I had spent the best part of a week peering into a bathroom mirror, crying, and trying to deny the undeniable truth: I had been lied to. I had lied to myself.

When I was not hiding in the bathroom during that fateful February, I was faced with freezing temperatures, even during the day, and when we visited friends in their post-Soviet apartment blocks, I had to step over great fallen columns of ice cut from the water pipes that ran down the outside of the grey crumbling structures. It did not feel safe. I did not feel safe. It was not safe. The streets reeked of decay. Weekly food banks had appeared under stern white canvas tents in certain parts of town, and rumour had it that food was being made available for a pittance by the Russian Oligarch who was soon to be Prime Minister, to compensate for the lack of money in the economy. This very same money, that he himself had doled out to various cultural, political, and social institutions, reduced to a trickle and then dried up altogether in a series of tit-for-tat moves between the ruling UNM party and the emerging Georgian Dream. In their game of political chess, the weaker pieces fell first; the elderly, the poor, and the dispossessed froze to death or starved. During previous visits, I had not noticed the acrimony I could now see being directed towards homosexuals and Muslims. Perhaps in the desperate days of that bitter February I was too preoccupied with survival to see it. However, as the week passed, I became more and more aware of the dangerous undercurrents of deeply ingrained hatred in this divided society.

I needed to get home quietly, without drawing attention to myself or arousing suspicion. I needed to put some distance between myself and my ex-lover, both geographically and emotionally. I also needed to cancel the choir's tour of the UK that we had been planning for later on that year. Cuts to arts funding in the UK were starting to hit, and sponsorship from private companies with a reason to promote Georgia had dried up, as they either went bust, or were taken over by bigger companies who had realised backing Georgia was not the most sensible business choice. When I wrote to people to tell them the 2012 tour was now cancelled, I elaborated on the desperate financial situation, and played down any personal grief. I think I managed to hide, or at least disguise, my own hurricane of emotions.

The embers glowed benignly as Keti and I talked deep into the night, accompanied by sips of blood-red Georgian wine, swirling in my best crystal glasses. We talked about the dark times, and she did her best to reassure me that I would be safe if I returned.

"You must understand," I said. "Georgia is like a boyfriend who shouts and sulks, who belittles and glares. Georgia makes me feel ugly and useless, and every time I think I understand him, he changes it all around, and manages to make everything my fault."

"Of course," Keti sighed. "Georgia is never, ever wrong."

When the morning of my return trip to Georgia finally arrived, my red-rimmed eyes were heavy with uncertainty. I tried to focus on the scribbles in my diary as I settled into my seat on the Gatwick Express. The short train journey was delayed by half an hour, due to a suicide, as it turned out. It felt like an omen, and the pit of anxiety I carried with me deepened. Slowing my breath deliberately, I closed my eyes and began to visualise already being in Georgia. I saw the cool, whitewashed walls of the church that overlooked Ananuri Lake, where I had swum and sang Shen Khar Venakhi, a beautiful ode to the Virgin Mary, with people I loved. I tried to hold onto memories of hot summer days, and adventurous summer nights during the first idyllic weeks with David. I did my best to fill myself with peace, not fear, but try as I might, the undeniable fact of the last moments of someone's life forever imprinted on the train-tracks filled me with foreboding. Bringing myself back and facing my fear, I opened my notebook, and added to the scribbles that already filled the page.

***

Trapped on the Gatwick Express

Death delayed me.

Splattered, matter-of-fact

Frazzled flesh

Diverted my travel thoughts

From

Cool lakes, hot white

Pavements and deep

Red wine to

Your

Final moments.

Flash of white

Before a lightning death.

3: An Unusual Event

The hot Tbilisi sunset stretches into purples and reds, and from where I sit, I can see the winking lights on the satellite mast that dominates the darkening night. Eliso, ever watchful, brings me frozen bottled water for my neck, wrists, and ankles. My feet are swollen, and I am glad for a chance to rest after our visit to the house on Erekle Street. My rucksack, always close now that it holds Nino's box, bumps against my calf, and I feel the reassuring corner of my treasure trove dig into my skin. Nino's diary, the pages slightly yellow in places, sits inside my own, larger clothbound diary, inviting me to read on. I try not to let on that I am doing anything unusual, hoping that, from behind, it looks as if I am reading and then scribbling, as usual.

***

July 18th 1918

Dear Diary,

Today, I am 14 years old! It has been the best day of my life. I am sorry I have not written to you for some time, but I have been so busy. Papa, dear Papa, has returned to us from the front. When I woke with the early dawn and looked into the garden, as usual, from my window, I could see the bent silhouetted figure of a man, picking Father's grapes and stuffing them into his mouth. Then I heard the cries, and Mother was there in his arms. I realised then it was Papa! There was crying and hushing as the lamps from next door's windows pooled dim light on the pathway. 'The Ottomans are nearly defeated,' he said and called for wine. I can hear them all singing and toasting and laughing. The garden is quite overrun with friends and neighbours, and Mother and Grand-Mama have been run off their feet preparing food all day.

I did not get to tend my garden today, of course. I was far too busy running errands and sending messages. Papa is home! I did not see much of him because he was resting and then the doctor came. I was surprised that Mother even noticed me trying to get out into the beds to check under the flowers. Once, I caught Haim looking at me through a chink in the wall and I hissed at him to go away. He is here now, down with the other men, toasting my father's return. I can hear his voice, floating up through the stifling night. It is a deep voice full of the earth and mountains. Why does he make me so angry? I think he knows about my little box of gold. I have found five more pieces in as many days! It is growing, as the flowers grow. Now that Papa is back, maybe I will tell him, or maybe I will wait a bit longer until I have enough to buy a diamond drop necklace.

He is handsome though, that Jewish boy Haim from next door. Papa does not like them. I overheard him and Grand-Papa arguing about it, but Grand-Papa says we can all learn a lot from one another. He said that one of God's greatest gifts is friendship and tolerance. Besides that, he says that now that we are Independent we can live, side by side, and anyway, someone has to keep Jason's gold coming down from the mountains. He laughs a lot when he talks about Jason's gold, and his eyes twinkle as he winks at me. Today he rubbed his stubbly cheek against my face and made me laugh. I hope he will remember I am 14 now, and start planning our trip to Europe.

Sweet dreams.

Nino

***

The night before I left for Georgia, it was stifling. The enclosed bellies of the London tube trains were unbearable and the suicide had time yet to change her mind. Keti, face grimed, shoe-pinched, plump and determined, slowed her pace as we neared the Georgian Embassy. Bits of stick stuffed in an Aldi bag clamoured for her attention amongst the tassels and beads, waiting to be transformed under her wrinkled fingers into a *gonja* doll.

I was there to learn about Nana, about Gaia, and Nino. I was there to see how this *gonja*, now with a dishcloth head and a body made of crossed rose bush stems, yellow buds discarded, could make it rain. I was there to hear how this doll with her jaunty swags and lace, so coy under her veils, beads and pearls, could sing her song and fracture the sky. I was there to sing, to dance. Ancient women's songs and ritual beckoned, and I was there to learn them. I wanted to learn Nino's Song.

So I sang, and as my voice joined with the others in the room, rising and falling, the thunder clouds gathered and pressed their purple noses against the white, high, square-paned windows. I danced. Nana, Gaia, Nino, and I awoke, and, with one heart beat ahead, and one heartbeat behind, we rejoiced as fat teardrops hit parched pavements.

***

Nino Sings to the Water

O Lazarus!
O Elijah!
Bring with you
Water for our drought.

See our feet, look how dirty they are
See how they tread the fertile land that groans
See how grain splits and pulses.

Bless our dolls, our gonja
We made them for you from
Cotton from your fields
Sticks from your trees
Beads and cowrie from your mountains that
Once sat at Nana's hearth.

See, we will return them to your rivers
We will stand and sing to you
We will sing your songs to the water.

We will sing and
Your grace
Will turn famine
To feast
And fill all our bellies.

Water Goddess!

Hear our song
Let it float, fuse
Your rushing torrents, swirl powerful eddies
And dance to our song, to our dream, to our
Wisdom.

To you
Our all
Our Nana.

4: *Sacrifice to Faith*

I can hear Nino and Eliso in the flat behind me, mixing ingredients into china bowls with silver spoons as they finally get to work making the cakes they had promised for the Tea Party the following evening. The heat trapped inside the flat bakes my back, even as the evening air flowing in from the window starts to cool my face. I am expecting over a hundred people, and I was beginning to wonder if the time Eliso spent talking about the cakes would be matched by time in the kitchen actually making them. "Can I help?" I call from my spot in the tiny sitting room, eyes still glued to Nino's diary. "No!" she calls back, breaking away from a seemingly unstoppable stream of gossip to answer. They are drinking wine and I hear giggling. Grumpy and feeling a little excluded, I slather on more *DEET* in an effort to prevent the mosquitoes from dive-bombing my blue-white skin, lit up like a runway by the single swinging bulb.

***

September 20th 1918

Dear Diary,

Today Papa gave me a rose bush, the most beautiful yellow climbing rose I have ever seen. He helped me plant it along the far wall where the sun is the strongest. I wanted to plant it next to the house, and Grand-Papa said it would thrive wherever we put it, but Papa insisted. 'The far wall,' he said, 'to fill that little gap into next door's garden.' Some of Mother's flowers had to be sacrificed, but she said she did not mind, and that a rose could be trained to cover more wall than any of her flowers ever could.

Haim was outside beating the sheepskins as we were planting. I saw his face through the gap as Papa tied the stems tight against it. One of the thorns tore at Papa's skin and he cursed under his breath and sucked his finger. Papa would never have cursed before the war. We ran out of twine, so he took one of my hair ribbons for the final tying. I began to protest, but he said I was getting too old for ribbons anyway. I would soon be quite the Young Lady!

Goodnight, dear Diary, I hope to have news about our trip to Vienna soon.

Nino

***

23

All those churning worries about coming to Georgia had, so far, been unfounded. Apart from a vague sense that I was never alone, neither he nor any of his cronies had shown their faces. Just 10 days ago, I was sitting in a café in the departure lounge at Gatwick airport, twisting the rings on my fingers until the skin went red, rehearsing my approach to ask security to let me out so I could leave and go home. The rising panic had set my feet twitching, and I imagined what would happen if I set the alarms off on purpose, or pushed against the tide of travellers that swarmed towards the neon-soaked shopping mall where I had just bought my new rucksack, in an attempt to exit through the main entrance. Just when I thought I was going commit a desperate act, I spotted a man completely engrossed in his book. He was just one person among the teaspoon-tapping clientele of the coffee shop. Something about the curve of his head caught my attention. I unclenched my hand and realised I hadn't been breathing.

***

The Reader

He, glasses absently slipping
Leans, back to the wall.

Feet up
Blue-heeled white socks crossed
In homage to the ancient art of
Reading
A
Book.

Inviting intimacy
He creates an oasis in the
Café's sea of sliding screens
Of individualism and
Electronic separation.

I scribble in my notebook
To join him.

5: Turbulence

"Leah, would you wash and pack the tea-cups and saucers for me, please?" Eliso calls from the kitchen. She has been collecting china teacups for weeks. Bric-a-brac market stalls have been raided, wedding sets donated, and gifts from friends collected. Friends and family have been co-opted into scouring antique shops ever since I first suggested an English tea party. Her treasure now lays scattered across her bedroom floor. "It has not been easy finding these in Georgia," she sighs as she hands me a cloth, "but somehow I have managed to find nearly one hundred cups." I look at them scattered on her bedroom floor, and realise that in the short time since she first gathered them, washed them, and dried them, the delicate rose pink and transparent blue white cups have already attracted a thin film of dust.

I sigh, and pick up the first cup. It's already past midnight. My dry eyes itch and I ache to sleep, but soon enough, I am in a rhythm: dip, wipe, wrap, pack, dip, wipe, wrap, pack. Wherever there is not a perfect match between cup and saucer, I do my best to couple up the colours; blue with blue, yellow with yellow. Failing that, roses seem to go well enough with swirls, and dotty cups attract chipped zig-zag saucers. It's almost 3 a.m. by the time I am done and can crawl into bed. I can't quite believe that in less than 36 hours I will be flying home. As much as half of me is dreading the Tea Party, the other half just wants to get it over and done with. I want to go home. From the kitchen, baked sponge smells drift out through open windows and up onto the acres of Soviet tower blocks and beyond, punctuated by intense mutterings and sharp, cutting commands. Along with the sound of thumping and a woman crying from somewhere close, my nerves tight wind ever tighter.

***

February 5th 1919

Oh dear God, it is so cold. This house is full of cracks and drafts, and my hands are numb, almost all of the time. The snow came yesterday, piles and piles of it, but last year's boots are too small so I cannot go outside. I am stuck in this old house and my hands are too cold even to play the piano. Grand-papa says he will mend a pair of Keti's old boots for me, tonight by the fire, after he finishes his work. This morning, Mother told me that it is best if I try not to think too much about going to Vienna as Papa is too sick to travel right now. Things are becoming more difficult because Mother is taking on more music students and Grand-Mama sighs a lot. It's harder for me to have time on the piano; there always seems to be someone else in our front parlour. Perhaps we can go to Vienna next year.

I have changed my hiding place. Keti was snooping around my room yesterday, and I am so frightened that if she finds my little box, she will tell Mother and then I will never see it again. There are quite a number of little nuggets of gold in there now, but I am sure they cannot be worth much. They are neither polished nor very beautiful in the cold blue light of my window.

Nino

***

The turbulence over the Turkish mountains was terrible. I spent a lot of time thinking about how I had arrived at this point. "Why are you returning to Georgia?" asked the older woman in the seat next to me. She had a kind face, tempered by a fierce fire in her eyes.

"Because if I don't, I will never be able to move forward." I replied.

She nodded and glanced at my diary, now filled with scribbles and sketches. "What are you working on?" she asked.

"I have been trying to sketch a timeline of the events that had brought me to this point in my life." I explained, showing her the knot of lines in soft pencil, with all but illegible scribbling beside them. She frowned. "I am trying to untangle a few things," I sigh, "but I am also wrestling with a re-write of a short story," I faltered glumly. "It's a work in progress."

"Yes, I see," she whispered. As the turbulence jolted us both, her blue-veined fingers gripped the armrest between us. "What happened here?" she asked, pointing to the single word *Corruption* next to the date February 2011.

"That's the story I am working on," I replied. My heart beat loudly and I suddenly felt afraid.

"Would it help if you read it to me?" she asked gently.

I nodded, took a deep breath, and began to read out loud.

***

Smoke swirls lazily into each corner of the third floor room. She watches the Chinese official light up another cigarette, the glow from the end of it contrasts sharply against the blue-white snow outside the window. Cold creeps along the floor, over the desk, and hunkers down in the creases of the crumpled bedding where she sits, waiting.

A steady stream of Chinese and Georgian interweave with ice-cold breath, and as she watches, the interpreter, a chunky young woman bundled up in woollen jumpers, jacket and scarf, switches languages effortlessly. The atmosphere thickens as the final details of the tour are thrashed out.

Watching them manoeuvre through the complex negotiations, she notices how he sits, this man of hers. He leans forward, twirling his mobile and constantly checking his watch. It makes her uneasy. She recognises the signs. She knows he is moving up a gear. She squirms. The desire to remain anonymous climbs in her like a wave, and she attempts, somehow, to disappear. Steam from damp clothing rises, joining the condensation on the window.

The drive to the isolated railroad company building high above Tbilisi had been full of unspoken tension and danger. Then, as now, she felt side-lined, hurried, manipulated, and hung out in a void of half-truths and shadowy half-finished conversations. During the drive, for the first time, his façade had really begun to slip. The dark smudges under his eyes framed a ruthless determination that she had only glimpsed briefly before. As spiteful criticisms thundered at her, she gave up trying to reason with him. When she said anything he did not want to hear, he deliberately swerved across the carriageway to frighten and silence her. It worked. Her throat was paper dry and it had taken every ounce of strength she had to stem the panic.

This new game, the one being played out in this freezing cold, smoke-filled seedy bedroom nauseates her. The snarling smiles and smirks sent her way by the short Chinese man, as well as the sideways glances from the interpreter, soon make it clear that business isn't the only thing they are talking about. She feels utterly humiliated. She is only in Georgia to be with him. She suddenly realises with a chill that being with him means doing whatever he wants her to do.

He is nervous. Things are not going well. He half stands, as if to leave, and there is a sudden flurry of activity. The official waves him back down furiously, picking up the phone on the desk opposite the bed. Urgent scribbling, paper already filled with doodles is soon also cluttered with numbers. He shakes his head each time. The official speaks more and more quickly into the receiver. Finally, there is a glance, just one, at her, and then past her. Then a half smile. The game is on.

He stands up to leave. Her head aches and she is confused. She waits for the right moment before she asks him what had happened. Smiling through tight lips, he tells her that tomorrow they return to sign an agreement. His choir will go on an all-expenses paid trip to China, where they will perform two 15-minute concerts. "That's great," she says, "the money can go towards our apartment in Tbilisi." The apartment block stood at the bottom of the plateau. He had bought it a few years before and showed it to her proudly. It was to be their marital home, he said. The apartment was unfinished, and as far as she could tell, no new work had been done on it for some time, despite him insisting it would be ready in plenty of time for them to move in. "It's the corruption," he said, by way of explanation.

He glances over at her expectant face. For a moment, she is hopeful, but then, his hollow laughter fills the car. "No," he sneers, "I will use this money for another project." She looks at his profile; he has turned the traditional folk music up on the radio, and is conducting with his right hand. She sits still and silent. The bleak white landscape stares back at her. All she can think about is getting home before he notices she is beginning to hate him. She needs to be able to pretend, at least until she can get out of the car, to mirror his false smiles and to do what he says.

They spend the rest of the afternoon driving around Tbilisi, him constantly on his phone arranging to meet various people who hand him passports and cash, out of earshot. The sky broods and threatens more snow as icy fingers of cold scratch their way into the car. She sits miserable, waiting and watching as he does his deals. He always has one foot on the curb, his shoulders hunch forward, and his hands are hidden deep in his pockets. Each time he looks at her, she smiles, nods encouragement, and dies a little more inside.

The next day, they go back to the smoke filled room where the stocky interpreter and the small Chinese man are waiting. This time the bed is made, but there are empty coffee cups on the windowsill that sit, like trapped cats, beside the dripping glass. Used tissues lie scattered on the floor. Documents are signed, hands are shaken. Sly smiles and dead eyes seal the deal. The choir will leave the following Friday. Visas need to be applied for, and quickly.

They are driven back into the city in a chauffeur-driven BMW, its cream leather interior imbued with cigarette smoke. She sits in the back feeling sick with hunger and realisation, while he, uninvited, assumes possession of the CD player, changing tracks frequently, much to the irritation of the driver. The Chinese embassy is expecting them, so they bypass the security checks. They sit at a wooden table in a room with emerald-green and fire-red dragons covering the walls. A solitary thick-leafed palm blocks light from the window.

He forges a signature for each document. She remembers the hours upon hours spent getting visas for him and his choir, and outrage builds inside her. Yet more forms are filled in, photocopies are taken, and official stamps are stamped. They drive, him victorious, her angry and resentful, to a bank in the city centre. Parking outside the low squat building, he tells her to stay in the car as he pays the money into his personal account, in cash.

The Chinese thought they were getting his choir, but they were getting five dancers and him. They were getting backing tracks, sleight of hand, and shadowy smiles. Illusion, collusion and manipulation hovers, mingling with fear. She breathes them in and tears prick her eyes.

She stays silent for a long time. When he finally notices her, there is a row. She is making him tired, he says. She does not understand how these things work, he claims. He has done all the work. He has negotiated the deal. Who would care if these dancers were part of his choir or not? The Chinese were pigs anyway. This was Georgia and he could do what he liked. The bitterness in his voice carry waves of anger that pin her to her seat. She watches as the final layer of deceit falls from his face. His features twist and his knuckles whiten as his hands grip the steering wheel.

Who is this man?

Glancing sideways, she realises she is a long way from home.

***

We cleared the mountains as I came to the end of the story. The woman took my hand in hers.

"Thank you," she said.

***

Thank-you

For keeping me   company - seasoned
Traveller.

You
Spoke of blood orange
      Sunrises over
Machu Picchu
And
Clattering Vietnamese
Bicycle spokes festooned with yellow-red-yellow ribbons
For lost   voice-
      less
Children.

Thank you
Great Adventurer, for
Your company, as my internal turbulence kept
My
Muttered prayers, twisting fingers, and shallow breath constant, urgent
Betrayed by fear.

'It's hard to stay

Grounded

When you

Are

So afraid,' I said.

You, blue-eyed woman who plays with

Radiotherapy, crinkle smooth blue-tinged skin, butterfly translucent smile, and with bent

Bejewelled fingers

Take my hand.

6: Imbecile!

I wake, in the early morning half-light to the sound of a mosquito buzzing. I reach for the cold metal of the flat-bladed silver knife to press against the swollen bitten skin of my red raw ankles. I sense, before I see, the bump of Eliso's body in the bed by the wall. Her handmade dress, all ready for the Tea Party, hangs on the front of the wardrobe, and I am humbled by her skills as a seamstress. It is a thing of beauty, covered with delicate patterns and fine stitching. It begs to be worn to some grand occasion, one where scented flowers adorn tables and the air is alive with sophisticated conversation. Seeing that dress, so full of expectation, makes me feel sad. I realise I cannot help Eliso. I cannot lift her from her poverty. I cannot save her from Georgia's crushing corruption, or even from her own pessimism. I cannot fix the endless flow of water through the cistern of her toilet or replace the cracked glass in her windows. I cannot stop her ex-husband threatening her, and I cannot pay her daughter's university fees. I cannot stave off the constant fear that her son will be conscripted as soon as he finishes his studies, and I am unable to listen to any more of the excuses she makes for the behaviour of her current boyfriend. As the scant relief afforded by the cold metal wears off, the mosquito buzzes once more past my left ear. I am left only with the cold realisation that I don't really understand her. Anything I can offer her is an illusion. The Tea Party is a distraction, that is all. The patch of mould that grows on the ceiling in the corner above her bed is blacker than before. I track the poisonous trail it leaves as drops of foetid liquid bubble through the plaster on her wall every time someone flushes a toilet upstairs. I lie on the rumpled bed, powerless. In less than 24 hours, I am leaving.

***

February 12th, 1919

Dear Diary,

The river was frozen today, so I went ice-skating. Mother let me use her skates - and they were divine - but even better than that, Haim was there! He looked amazing in his thick woollen chokha, like an upside down triangle. None of the other boys were nearly as handsome, and when he smiled at me and offered me his arm, we skated round and round. If I closed my eyes for a moment, I could imagine we were at a great ball, I in a gown the colour of the sun. We glided across the marble floor like elegant swans. As the light faded, and Haim and I stood for a moment in the steel grey dusk, he picked up a pebble and skipped it across the ice. The sound rang out and created the purest of notes that wrapped themselves around the evening air. Delighted, he threw another pebble. The sounds echoed through the air, dancing together and filling the valley. I felt my heart leap. Could it be that I am falling in love?

When I returned, Papa and Grand-Papa were fighting again. Grand-Papa said Social Federalism was a good thing, a noble thing, and I heard him call Papa a Bolshevik. Then he stormed out of the house. Papa is sitting now, brooding in the front parlour, and poor Mother has had to cancel her piano lessons.

Perhaps, when the ice and snow melt, everything will return to normal.

Goodnight.

Nino

***

I lay in the growing light, my mind preparing itself for the journey home. I found myself thinking about the second leg of my journey, from Ankara to Tbilisi. My memories were dominated by a conversation with a corpulent Turkish man in his 50s, with blue stubble and a shirt collar a few sizes too tight. He was the CEO of one of Georgia's newly-built power stations, and, at first, he seemed pleasant and I felt safe enough. I flashed my hands at him ostentatiously from the outset of our conversation to make sure he got the message; I was wearing a fake wedding ring and engagement ring on both hands. The last thing I wanted was any of *that* kind of attention. As the journey wore on, our chat moved inevitably beyond swapping pleasantries, and we strayed into political and social discussions about Georgia. I was suddenly aware that he was leaning in just a little bit too close, his right arm encroaching on my personal space just that little bit too much. In spite of me telling him (quite pointedly, I thought, twisting my array of fake marriage jewellery on pale fingers) about my son and the rest of my family earlier, he had clearly made his mind up that I was vulnerable, and therefore, available.

"Your husband, he is waiting for you in Tbilisi?" he asked, one bushy eyebrow raised. That eyebrow signalled a shift. Quite suddenly, a perfectly intelligent and reasonable conversation transformed into a series of irritating, and potentially inflammatory, misunderstandings. Why is it that when a woman says no, it is seen as the beginning of a negotiation?

I say, "I love exploring and experiencing new cultures and people."

You think I say, "Before I sat in this seat next to you, there was nothing interesting in my life."

I say, "The songs of Georgia move me, haunt me."

You think I say, "I am a slave to my emotions and do not know my own mind."

I say, "I have been hurt by Georgia, but I am trying to forgive her."

You think I say, "I am waiting to be rescued by a strong man, who is not Georgian."

I say, "I am saddened by the way women are treated in Georgia."

You think I say, "Can I visit you in Turkey, so I can see how a real woman should behave?"

I say, "I am tired; it has been a long day."

You think I say, "Of course you can wipe the smudged mascara from under my eye with your spit-moistened thumb."

I say, "Well, thank-you for your company and interesting conversation on this flight."

You think I say, "Thank-you for giving me your business card. I will call you and we can have meaningless sex."

I say, "Goodbye and good luck."

You think I say, "Please can you take my hand-bag and my rucksack from me, and carry it through the entire terminal until we get to passport control, because I've been waiting for someone to relinquish my identity to."

I think, "You knob." But instead, I smile. Tightly.

I say, "Goodbye."

But still, you ask me to call you, your sweaty palm pressed into mine. I do not smile. I say nothing. Your eyebrow twitches at me.

Perhaps you will excuse me then, if to make things simpler, I say, "Look, just FUCK OFF!" So there is no chance for your continued

Misunderstanding.

I straightened my back, held my head high, squared my jaw and took my bag from him, resisting the urge to look around me for back-up. It was 4 a.m. and I was in passport control at Tbilisi airport, surrounded by people I did not know, and unsure whether my friend and translator Eliso would be in the arrival hall waiting for me. The man recoiled from me in shock, as though he had been bitten. As the oppressive heat from outside seeped into the cavernous space, I moved purposefully towards passport control. I jumped the queue, pushed forward, jostled, and stood my ground. I squared my hips and back-blanked the predator who stood silent at the white line dividing the hopeful from the hopeless. Passing through past unsmiling guards without incident, back straight in triumph, I waited for my suitcase. He, luggage-less, scurried towards his waiting Mercedes. He spat a word at me as he passed, "Bitch".

Through the white gates I could see a crowd of expectant faces, one of which, pale and round, belonged to Eliso. I grabbed what I believed to be my new red oversized suitcase from the turtle-shell carousel and, with a tightening chest, walked into the morning dazzle of Tbilisi.

***

Lost Luggage

4 a.m.

Humid morning heat

Heads cluster as

Faces seek stories from foreign lands.

I trundle

Behind me the duplicitous

Doppelgänger suitcase

Holding nothing of necessity for this particular life.

7: Can I trust you?

As the morning wears on, my fingers itch to explore the golden objects in the box. So far, it has been easy to hide Nino's little book inside the pages of my own diary, but the box is bulkier, so it stays nestled into the front pocket of my rucksack. Even though Eliso's apartment has several cavernous rooms, there are always a lot of people there – uncles, cousins, sons, neighbours – drifting up and down the long central corridor and disappearing through the dark wooden doors on either side. The only real privacy to be found is in the dank dripping bathroom, and I don't want to spend too much time in there. The washing machine bounces around the floor, cracking ancient Wedgwood blue tiles with every thud. Frayed wires trail across the walls, swing from damp pipes, and loop over the shower head. Their various torturous paths all lead, eventually, to the two scorched electrical sockets by the door.

"I am just going to the little market to get some things," I say quietly to Eliso, recently emerging, blinking and yawning, from her snoring sleep, still cocooned in her blankets. She is too bleary to protest, managing nothing more than a vague look of alarm through eyes swollen from baking cakes throughout the night. Today is the day of the Tea Party. As I leave, I see her first attempt at getting up fail, and hear her sigh as I close the front door. I negotiate the dim hallway, rummaging in my pocket for a five tetri coin to pay the coffin-like lift to convey me to the ground below. I sling my rucksack casually over my shoulder. The book within the box shifts inside.

***

May 28th 1919

Dear Diary,

I am worried about Papa. He is so sick. The house must be kept quiet and cool for him, and the piano lessons have stopped. The only sound from outside comes from Haim next door. There is the usual beating of the skins, and some hammering, but Papa rages at it and nothing Mother can do calms him. Grand-Papa is working such long hours at the university, I hardly get to see him, and Mother and Grand-Mama creep around like mice. Mother is thin and grey, while Grand-Mama gets plumper and plumper. My headaches come and go, but no one seems to care if I grind my teeth anymore. Keti spends all her time studying, and I try to tend the garden whenever I can. I cut some yellow roses today and put them in Papa's room. He smiled at me, but his smile was sad and empty. I left without saying very much.

I made a cutting of Papa's rosebush and planted it by the house wall under my window today. Haim helped me. He helps us a lot now. We don't talk that much, but I hear him sing sometimes at night, and it soothes me a little. I want the rose to grow and cover the crumbling stone of our house. I want to smell the sweet scent every morning. It helps my aching head.

I asked Mother's permission before I planted the cutting, but she seemed not to hear me and waved me away. There is sickness in our house this year, and no matter how often I look under Mother's flowers, I never see a hint of gold.

Goodnight

Nino

***

My first morning in Georgia did not start well. Eliso and I had planned to catch the early morning train to Batumi. I, however, was reluctantly playing the 'I have to wait for my missing luggage to arrive' game, so I was faced with an unplanned stay in Tbilisi. Eliso's flat was directly opposite the office where David worked for a radio broadcaster. My trip to Georgia was a closely guarded secret, and the intention had been to whisk me in and out of the city in the early hours before David arrived at work, just in case. Now, here I was, just 25 yards from where he worked, clearly visible to anyone who chose to look up if I happened to be passing too close to the window. My thoughts of him, and of the times I had been to his studio, hung heavily in my mind. I tried to ignore the memories of the many times I had spent learning, recording, loving and being loved in return - or so I thought. It made my heart ache. Memories of his voice, his breath, the way he walked, and his particular scent, sweet and musky, rose to the meet me as the heat of the day intensified. His friend, Ramaz worked with him as a sound engineer. Ramaz was my friend too. We three had laughed and giggled through several frozen February days in front of a three-bar electric heater, faces ablaze and backs frozen, but deliciously snug in the security of our friendship and love.

"I want to see Ramaz," I told Eliso.

She laughed, "Keep watching from that balcony, and you will see him soon enough."

I hoped Ramaz was someone I could trust. He had remained a friend to both of us despite everything that had happened. I knew he might be with David, but I called anyway. The phone rang three times before he answered in his familiar gruff tones. "It's me, Leah," I said, "Come to the front of the building in ten minutes. I will meet you outside."

***

Peering Around Corners

You arrive, all smiles and bear-hugs.
Joyful resonant laugher and puckered laughter lines
Betray dismembered memories.

You peer around corners with eyes
That look on parallel worlds
Upstairs
Through doorways
Threads in time fracture
We pass a memory.

Once, we three
Hid in that cupboard, played hide-and-seek with
Authority, avoided confrontational conversation with
Anzor Erkomaishvili. You, naughty boy, doubled up, snorting and guffawing
Reached for your handkerchief to
Wipe silent tears. He, with so much to lose
Stood silent, ear cocked, waited as his future self
Passed.

I, drunk on giggles
Reached out, found fear
Withdrew.

We climb wide granite stairs wrapped
In stern railings
Up, up
Quick steps above us

You call the shots
Salute a stop
Peer around corners.

I wait.
We pass a memory
Once, we three
Walked this path as
Flickering damp February
Lights hid underfoot fractures.

We huddled in the neverlight glow
Of the artificial mainframe
As steaming clothes and
Cooked calves pirouetted with
Heaven-sent Chakrulo
That old illusionist.

Omnipotent radio-wave voice
Slices through memories to fill
Me with fresh lies.

Your shoulders relax
We are on solid ground.

Now, we drink English tea
From pretty china cups
Pretend to be happy
Just the two of us.

8: Only God Can Judge Me

A wall of heat hits me the second I leave the tower block. It is so hot, I struggle to breathe. Immediately to my right, there is a cold water pipe gushing liquid silver into a cracked and yellowing pot sink sitting between two ancient trees that cast cool pools of shade. Two old men in brown trousers perch on a wall and smoke. The water sparkles, casting irregular segments of diamond light on the rust-addled wall of a decrepit shed that spills watermelons from its open doors onto the ruined tarmac. A woman dressed in black sits, already weary, her back a shadowed oblong between the scorching morning sun and the baked-metal shade of her hut.

I seek a shady spot where I can sit and look, for the first time, at the treasures in Nino's box. I finally find a bench on the corner of Tkvarcheli Street, plunged in the gloom under the heavy branches of venerable trees reaching across to one another over the pot-holed carriageway. A bric-a-brac shop hunkers down on the corner directly opposite me, filled with faded carpets, dented cooking pots, old shoes, books, and pictures of Stalin in all shapes and sizes. The largest likeness of this Georgian dictator sits in Technicolor, pride of place on the pavement in his own chipped golden frame, itself framed against a rich red and blue rug, majestically hung. His image dominates the street. My courage evaporates under his stern glare, and I leave the box in my bag. Instead, I hurry to the market and buy fruit for breakfast. The peaches are soft and the grapes firm. The dumpy woman in floral skirts bubbles with good natured amusement as I ask her, using lots of hand gestures and crinkly-eyed smiles, to slice the watermelon for me. I amuse her in general, it seems. She over-charges me. I stop by at the hole-in-the-wall bakery, and buy Tsintsadze's black bread: my favourite.

***

July 17ᵗʰ 1919

Dear Diary,

My fortunes have changed! Today, I found the most beautiful golden locket I have ever seen under my climbing rose, tucked in behind Mother's flowers. It is tiny and has delicate swirling patterns on it that seem to trickle like water across mountain stream stones. Inside is my name alongside one other: Haim's.

It is my birthday tomorrow, and the day after that, we celebrate Keti's wedding. She is 18 and is marrying a Russian boy called Alexei. He is a soldier. I think she is nervous, and I know it is not a love-match, but Papa says it is time, and as he is the son of an old army friend and from a good family, she will learn to love him. I wonder what it is like, to be married. I want to marry for love, not for any other reason. Not because Papa says I must.

Goodnight.

Nino

***

It took six hours to travel to Batumi from Tbilisi by train. As the carriages trundled through the countryside, the windows framed scene after dramatic scene of formidable mountains topped by cloud, dry arid plains, lush fields of green, and old crumbling apartment blocks with cracked windows and leaking pipe-work. Disused railway lines ran parallel, and lead inevitably to Gori, Stalin's birthplace. The whole region reeked of disappointment. I saw, through petrol-coloured train windows, weed-infested sidings that wept as they remembered. Eliso shook a bag full of homemade cinnamon swirls under my nose. Reaching in, a trail of icing sugar tracked across my clothes, a distraction from the abandoned destruction outside. Licking the sickly sweet sugar from my lips, I glanced around me.

No-one else seemed to be looking out of the window. No-one else seemed to care.

***

Cinnamon Swirl

I see

An ancient land

It dwarfs us.

Low plain

Meandering sacred river turns to

Tributaries that tighten like

Veins

Towards Stalin's square.

He waits

Rusted

Cattle trucks

Open to destruction, retch

Ghosts and bullet-hole memories onto

Disfigured lands.

His resurrection imminent

He just waits.

Disillusioned, I eat

Crescent moon cinnamon swirls, the colour of sunshine that

Melt, all distracting butter, in my mouth.

***

Our arrival in Batumi at 12 p.m. was eventful in that the taxi driver threw us out of the car, before we got to our accommodation. Eliso and he exchanged increasingly heated words, as she, mobile phone glued to her ear, peered into the darkness, searching for the voice that spilled from the receiver. He finally admitted he did not know where he was going, and stopped suddenly. Scurrying like a rat, shoulders stooped, cigarette glowing, he opened the boot and dumped our bags on the pavement. He wrenched my door open and almost before I could put both feet on the ground, jumped back behind the wheel and sped off, cursing.

We were lost. With only the tinny voice from the mobile phone to guide us, and accompanied by some leery comments from pavement drinkers, we walked silently until we caught sight of a large woman draped in a bold floral print, who waved at us, frantically. The woman was the owner of the apartment Eliso had rented for our stay in Batumi, and with a dismissive wave of her hand and a hiss through her teeth, she passed judgement on all taxi drivers. Safe inside, we drank tea and planned for tomorrow.

Batumi is a playground for the rich: rich Georgians, rich Russians, rich Turks. It is half-heartedly developed and half-heartedly broken-cobble abandoned. Modern architecture clashes with traditional tree-lined avenues. The next morning we sat, on the shoreline, having walked through pockets of heat to lounge under tender blue skies with our feet dipped in the Black Sea.

***

Batumi

White, white Batumi
You rise, shake off flint grey
Pebble sounds.

A shoreline of blue heartbeats that pause, skip
Genuflect
To the majesty of

Your mountains
A snow-white spine upon which
You hang.

***

I enjoyed those lazy few hours on the Batumi beach during which time we ate soft, golden boiled corn, and bags of juicy cherries and peaches. I watched people playing in the water and standing on the shoreline. One man caught my eye, his entire back covered in tattoos, underneath a phrase spanning from one shoulder blade to the other like the title of a book. It read, in English, Only God Can Judge Me.

I wanted to talk with him. I wanted to strike up a conversation about the scenes of hell and damnation that danced on his stretched flesh, giving warning of the coming Apocalypse. Was he an Orthodox priest, I wondered? Did all priests wear such a vestment under their robes that pricks, burns, and scars like a modern-day hair shirt? I tucked my legs away under the shade of the umbrella as my pale skin reddened, and gazed upon the scenes of damnation the man wore so effortlessly.

***

Only God Can Judge Me

Declares the tattoo across the
Back of the man who
Stands firm upon these pebble shores.

Flesh sears as the folding skin
Signs of excess roll down
Sit
Paunchy atop
Tight red trunks.

Incense burning saints command attention and flinch
As shoulder blades burn.

They crave cool dark
Cavernous vestments of the
Interior.

Your omnipotent message impregnates.

Violates.

Soils.

I stare, you turn, and our eyes meet.

Your tongue flicks as
I bite deep into the dribbling flesh of an overripe peach.

***

Eliso was laughing. "Don't," she sniggered, "there are already too many budgies in his pants. You must not encourage him."

I bit defiantly into my peach and glanced reluctantly at my tablet. I had a stack of reading I wanted to do about Saint Nino. "I am feeling so lazy," I said. "Can you tell me everything you know about Saint Nino? Apart from the fact that she looks as if she has been kidnapped and imprisoned on that man's back."

Eliso feigned shock, "You know she is our greatest Saint. You know she brought Christianity to Georgia in the third century and you know the church teaches us to be like her?"

"Hmmmm," I reply, flicking through the pages of the *St. Nino Quarterly* online. I read about how her story was re-written by the Georgians in the 10th century to suit the patriarchal ideal of woman. "Did you know that St. Nino played a significant role in the actual baptism of the royal family in the third century? I mean, she actually baptised them herself, rather than the Greek priests who had been sent to do the job?" I asked Eliso, who was getting redder and redder under the burning sun.

"This cannot be true," Eliso mumbled from beneath her sunglasses. "Only men can do that."

I pushed the tablet under her nose until she paid it some attention. Her eyes flicked left to right a few times and then her eyebrows shot up. She scratched her head, reading about a vision Nino had in which Mary explained to her that men and women were equal. "This would explain why Nino travelled and preached. I always wondered how she could do these things back then, when the church today says we cannot." Eliso suddenly narrowed her eyes and glared at me. "It's propaganda," she said.

"Either that," I replied, "or this information has been erased on purpose by a church that wants to keep women silent."

Eliso handed me my tablet back and looked away out to the blue horizon. She settled back on her sun lounger, and glanced at the tattooed man now strutting up and down the shore line. I was sure I heard her mutter, "Bastard," under her breath. I wasn't sure if it was meant for him or for me.

9: Lessons in the Absurd

Tsintsadze's bread is warm and its earthen smell fills the endlessly-swinging, *tetri*-hungry lift that I take to the ninth floor and Eliso's apartment. Juddering to a stop at the fifth floor, I am joined by another woman. We look at each other in the dark glow of the orange light. She wears sunglasses. A large Saint Nino's cross on a silver chain nestles between her breasts. Neither the sunglasses nor the cross cover the yellowing bruises that spread, like ink stains, under her skin.

***

July 19th 1919

Dear Diary,

The wedding was beautiful. Sioni was lit with candles, and the icons watched us from every wall. Keti and Alexei wore the crowns, gold filigree adorned with pearls and jewels. They walked the circle of love three times anti-clockwise, as strains of sacred music and holy marriage songs sung by a local choir rang out. All of our family, friends, and neighbours were there. Haim kept me close to him and made sure I could see everything, feel everything. He smiled into my eyes, and as Keti and Alexei moved towards the sacred steps that women can climb only on their wedding day, he turned to me and said, 'Please God let that soon be you.'

Did my heart hear right? Does he want to marry me? I must have looked shocked because he smiled and leant towards me, whispered into my ear, 'Let us be married before the summer ends.' Something inside me spun, Papa would never allow it, but Grand-Papa would understand. We were Independent after all, and our society was based on openness and tolerance. Perhaps there was some hope for us.

There were lots of soldiers on the streets of Tbilisi today, and as we walked from the church back home for the wedding supra, Papa and Alexei spent some time talking and drinking with them. Keti was all brown eyes and trembling lips. Earlier this morning, I had given her one of my yellow roses pressed between the pages of a book containing the words from our greatest poet, Shota Rustaveli. Her long fingers had shaken as she placed them on the top of her trunk.

She will be leaving us today. Tomorrow she will wake up a married woman in another house.

Haim and I slipped away once the heavy drinking and dancing began, and walked hand-in-hand under the stars. We were by the river when he gave me a golden chain. 'I made it myself,' he said as he held my hair up as I fastened the chain around my neck. 'It's for your locket.' I felt him watching me. I fumbled just a little and he held my hand gently, guiding it to the crook of his arm. Then, like the perfect gentleman, he walked me home.

I only just made it back before Papa noticed I was gone, but Grand-Papa was smoking in the front garden and met my eyes as I moved past him. He tapped me under my chin with one hand and held my shoulder tight with the other. 'Shining eyes,' he said, 'I am happy for you. I am happy for you.' He caught me by the waist and spun me around like he did when I was a child. 'Come rejoice in her brightness! Gaze at will on her beauty!' he shouted to the moonlight. I laughed out loud at his joy, and mine.

Soon, Grand-Papa will speak with Mother about Haim, and Haim will speak with Papa. Please let them see that this love is good and pure. Please let them see. Please let them see.

Goodnight.

Nino

***

After our day of sunshine and shade on the Black Sea shoreline, Eliso and I were walking back towards our apartment when we passed an imposing Gothic-style cathedral. A sign outside proclaimed, proudly, in Georgian, English, and Russian, that whilst the building had originally been built for Catholic worship, it was now Georgian Orthodox.

"Shall we see if Saint Nino dwells within?" Eliso asked, a twinkle in her eye?

In every incense and shadow-filled recess, a saint lurked, watching us. With no sign of St. Nino, other eyes followed us as we moved quietly between vast stone columns. A priest approached Eliso and muttered at her in urgent, hushed tones. She flushed dark with fury. We had been asked to leave.

Eliso's defiance burned hard on her cheeks. Glancing up, I caught sight an image of St. Nino, all but hidden in a dark corner, suddenly bathed in a shaft of light. Motes, suspended in the stale air, danced around her, creating a halo which stretched, like a beacon into the cavernous vaults above.

"Do you want to leave?" I asked my friend, once the priest had sulked off.

"Absolutely not," she replied. "Why should we? He thinks women should live in the past, but he," she paused before spitting the last words out, "wears a Rolex watch, drives a jeep, and watches women sweep dust from stone floors with brooms made from twigs! Bastard."

***

St. Nino is a Feminist

Cool dark interior offers
Sanctuary.

Icons, golden, watchful, green-eyed and glinting steel
Flickering candle light, move
Watching eyes
Into hidden guilty corners.

From the sea we had come. Had
Bathed in her glorious waters
Sung our songs to her
Soaked the golden light from her and
Healed.

Legs and shoulders covered, hips hidden
Heads bowed, we held ourselves close as
Damp parts of our private
Memories evaporated.

Unseen cradled breasts, swimsuit crotches
Hidden under layered clothing
Steamed.

The jailer

His black beard

Black dress, sandals padding on ancient stone floors

Dark triumphant roaming eye

Approved by watching

Masters,

Asked us to leave.

'It is not allowed to enter this sacred space on the way to, or from bathing,'
he said.

'Do you think St Nino did this? Think carefully.

We must do all we can to preserve traditions'

My quick-tongued companion replied

'Think about it yourself

Do you think St. George drove a jeep?'

St. Nino smiled from dark corners

Bowed to the wisdom of all women

Sang her songs

To the water.

***

I moved away from the ugly whispers directed at us from the priest who had returned, uninvited. I stood just inside the doorway to the outside world, and looked out onto the street. I saw a gaggle of brown-skinned girls, all legs and shining white teeth. They gathered in front of the outer gate of the church under the shade of an oak tree, bouncing against one another in their eagerness to be seen by the priests guarding the entrance. They crossed themselves quickly, giggled and sped off, heels kicking up black volcanic dust from the shoreline.

I squared my shoulders, lifted my head high, unwound my headscarf, took a swig of water from my bottle, freed my hips from the extra sarong and escaped into the sunshine outside.

10: Trust my Magic, Music, and Power

I walk back into chaos, the memory of the woman's bruises fresh in my mind; to an apartment that is awash with women. Eliso's cousin and best friend from Kutaisi have arrived. There is whipped cream and sliced peaches in bowls on every available surface in the kitchen, and the soft sweet scents assail my senses. Eliso sits with cold compresses over her eyes and barks out an order every time she lifts her head from the kitchen table. Her commands are studiously ignored; they are the cavalry and they know what to do. They look at me with side-smiles as I enter the kitchen.

"For goodness sake, give me a job to do!" I exclaim. A guttural noise emerges from somewhere deep inside Eliso and I am immediately herded out, down the long corridor, into the back bedroom and onto the far balcony. As a guest, I am not allowed to lift a finger. I am a gift from God. So I sit. I see a little shrine in the corner of the balcony. It consists of a few bits of Eliso's art work, some seashells, a wilting plant in dire need of a good watering, and a picture of St. Nino. My frustration mounts. My rucksack is close to my feet but I dare not take the box out. I can almost hear St. Nino's whispering voice in the breeze, too light to offer respite from the heat. I reach inside my rucksack and take out my purse instead. Inside, tucked into a little pocket is a three-fold portable shrine. I open it. On the left is King David IV the Builder. He saved Georgia in the 10th century. In the middle is the Virgin Mary and the Baby Jesus, and there, on the right is St. Nino. Her long dark hair falls over her shoulders and her sanguine smile suggests there is more to her than her saintly halo might suggest. I carry her everywhere I go.

"Go lightly, go well. Go with my magic, my music and my power." Her magic moves the leaves on Eliso's dying plant with a rustle, and the hairs on my arms respond and rise.

Suddenly Eliso is here.

"Come," she commands. "I must go to the salon and have my nails done. You can meet your friend first, and then Ramaz will host you until we are ready for this evening." I return St. Nino to her place in my purse, scoop up my bag and, strangely excited at the prospect of being an independent traveller today, I forget about the fear that lies in the pit of my stomach.

***

November 5th 1919

Dear Diary,

Haim has gone! His family have sent him to Svaneti to oversee the family business and I miss him terribly. Before he left, he built a grand pergola under my window so my yellow rose could grow tall. He is such a good man. Now, instead of under the flowers, I found golden pieces on my windowsill. My collection is growing. Two days ago I found a little turtle with bright red rubies on its back and emerald green stones for its eyes. Haim also made me a blue velvet lined box to keep all my treasures in. The outside is made of ebony and ivory and it has the smallest key-hole with a tiny key made of gold that I wear with my locket. I am wearing high-necked dresses now that I am nearly 16, so Mother cannot see.

Grand-Papa never spoke to Mother. Haim never spoke with Papa, either. Within a few weeks of Keti's wedding, there was so much trouble on the streets of Tbilisi that everyone returned to their homes and the shutters went up on the windows and doors. Soldiers from the Red Army seem to be everywhere. Grand-Papa is busy organising protests at the university, writing pamphlets, and giving speeches about how important it is to remain Independent. I hardly get to see him anymore. I would like to go out with him and tell people to join the Democratic Party, but this just makes Papa angrier. Haim says I must stay quiet and keep watch, that I must tell him what I see and hear in the house and on the streets. I don't want to betray Papa like that, so I stay silent. When Grand-Papa is not here, the house is full of Alexei's soldiers. They are loud and demanding. This is the only time I see Papa happy. Mother and Grand-Mama have been saving food and fuel, just in case we have a winter like last year.

Come back Haim, quickly please.

Goodnight.

Nino

***

Eliso and I had met up with Nino the ethnomusicologist, the evening before we were due to travel to Zugdidi in Samegrelo province. We drank wine in a white swanky Batumi square whilst a string quartet played to the golden rays of the dying sun, and chatted about Nino's plans to visit as many women as possible, so that we could hear their stories and learn about their traditions and cultures. I liked Nino's plan and I readily agreed.

What I did not realise was that no one had thought about how we would travel to these places. On previous visits, I had the luxury of David's car, but this time, public transport was the only option.

My guide-books agreed gloomily that people die in road accidents all the time in Georgia, and that white public mini-buses ought to be avoided at all costs. Even Eliso had raised an eyebrow when Nino suggested them as the best way of travelling from Batumi to Zugdidi. The next morning, when I found myself being herded into a white mini-bus that would carry me through mountains above roaring rivers, my bravado from the night before had evaporated. I was too frightened most of the time to do anything other than dwell in ever-more morbid detail on my impending violent end. I clutched at my own hands and bit my lips to stop myself shaking and whimpering like a child, as the view from the grimy window revealed sheer drop after sheer drop.

***

White Mini-Bus of Doom

I remember
The story of a
Beautiful woman who
With her unborn child in her belly
And another by her side
Drowned.

They fell into a ravine on a mountain-pass
Entombed in a mini-bus.

I heard the rattle of
Her
Last. Gasping. Breath.

The final clutch of sodden fabric that
Ripped as her first born was
Sucked
Into the frothing swirl.

I follow her route.

I sit in her seat.

I tremble
And give my journey to God.

***

As my stomach lurched in time with the thrum of the engine over crumpled tarmac. My mind wandered, transporting me back to my second visit to Georgia. I was being hosted by David and his family, and we were at home. As usual, his mobile phone was glued to his ear, but this time, I could tell something was very wrong. I watched as his face drained of colour. He hung up and sank onto the floor. He gripped my hand as he told me what had happened.

Her life story was well known. Young, beautiful, gifted, and from one of the oldest singing families in Georgia, she had moved, with her husband, to a remote region, turning her back on fame, to live a natural life away from any 'bad' influences. She had been an inspiration to female folk singers around the world, and inspired by her voice, I was doing my best to learn a solo piece she had recorded earlier that month. She had the most harmoniously haunting voice, rich and mountainous, full of black grapes and ochre soil. Now she was dead. Through his tears, David picked up his car keys and left. He was going to see the family. He did not come back for three days.

I am no stranger to loss. My father died when I was 22 and the grief never disappeared. Instead, life grew around it. If I catch sight of dad's handwriting on the cards I kept, or smell the scent of a cherry cigar, or hear a particular song on the radio, it transports me back to that moment when I screamed to the heavens, "Take me instead". I learnt death will not to be bargained with. They hold death close in Georgia. They submit completely to the eventuality of it. In theory, at least, the soul goes to a better place, and those left behind have an elaborate array of rituals designed to keep them connected to the dead in order to remember and honour them. Families gather at the grave to eat, drink, toast, share stories, cry, laugh, and accept their loss regularly as the years tick by. The dead are welcome too at the feasting table, named in the supra toasts alongside those still living.

I got to witness Georgian grief first hand once, during one of the UK tours I had organised for the choir. All twelve of them were staying at my house, but I was looking forward to a quiet day where I had some space. I wanted to use the washing machine and walk the dog. I had not seen my son for a while, as the tour had kept me away, and I was happy to be home. He was only 13 at the time, and I was aware that there had been some interest in how 'manly' he was from the men in the choir, accompanied by some well-intentioned, but unwelcome 'male role-modelling' going on. They were overly boisterous, dangerously physical, and claustrophobically matey, assuming he would prefer to drink and eat with them rather than with me. It was difficult for an only child, and just as I felt I had to intervene, he fled, keeping himself to himself in his converted loft room. It was his sanctuary.

As I folded the washing in the sunny back room on this particular afternoon, I was suddenly aware of a change of atmosphere in the house. Everything went quiet and grey.

David called me downstairs, and when I got into the kitchen, all twelve of them were standing there, each holding a glass of red wine, stock-still, solid and unmovable. When the toasts began, the men were quiet, respectful, emptied out of bravado and ego. In its place there was pain, loss, hurt, and displacement. This particular ritual was for a fallen member, a man who had died in 2009. They told me he had been the best of them. He had left behind a young wife and two very small children. I had been to his grave in Tbilisi. It was a haunting and haunted place, and I had felt like an intruder. That bitter February day in 2010, I had felt the iron railing, cold in my hand, and wondered at the stone benches, the picnic table, felt the wind buffer the elevated and gravelled space, uncompromising and stern. That same sense of intrusion settled over me again, now permeating my own home. On the anniversary of this man's death, they did not want to be standing in my kitchen any more than I wanted them there, with their eyes full of pain and their endless forever-grief. It was not because I did not care, but because I felt like I was never going to be allowed in enough to show them that I did care. Their grief was not private, but neither was it public. It was exclusive and dismissive of anything I might have to offer them.

Four hours in a white mini-bus, as it traversed the tiny, neglected roads, kept my breath short and my chest tight. As we entered the miniature city of Zugdidi those feelings lessened. I looked out at benign summer rivers and fields of ripening crops, grateful for the open window that forced air into my lungs and kept me alive, despite the suffocating fear. Like relief solidified, Zugdidi welcomed us with wide white tree-lined boulevards, shimmering faded café fronts, and glimpses of civilisation present, and past. I wondered what lay ahead.

11: Today I Drank Water from the Well

The ever-present smog clings to our clothes and skin. Eliso hands me over to Ramaz, bundling me into a beaten up taxi with lumpy seats. I may be uncomfortable but at least I am away from the Tea Party preparation stress back at the flat. My throat constricts as we head for Sameba Cathedral, and I wonder if, by the time the evening comes, I will be able to speak at all. The taxi lurches like a boat on the high sea, and the driver lights yet another cigarette. I try to open the window, but the handle is broken. Ramaz comes to the rescue with gesticulation, posturing, and lip pursing, finally pressuring the driver into making do with breathing in the polluted air inside the cab, instead of adding yet more smoke to it. He grins a toothless grin, opens the door briefly to a rush of noise, and tosses the butt onto the street with a shrug. Broken cobbles add to the relentless swaying as we negotiate narrow causeways. I gulp breaths of stale air and hold onto the contents of my stomach. I know Ramaz will have made sure David is not singing today, but still my knees feel weak. With blurry eyes and cold shaking hands, it seems as good a time as any, so I swallow hard and ask, "Why did David do what he did to me?"

Ramaz sighs and in broken English, his brown eyes full of concern, replies, "I don't understand him. I tell him to love his friends, be friends first before marriage, friends like you are." I can tell this is tearing Ramaz apart, so I choose not to press him further and wait for the streets to open up into opulent gardens and sandstone shrines. St. Nino is in Sameba, and I want to talk to her.

***

April 9th 1920

Dear Diary,

I was awakened this morning by the sound of gravel being thrown against my window. I peered down, and saw Haim looking up at me. I opened my window so he could climb up. Almost as soon as I had unlatched it, he was there and in my room. I was so worried Papa would hear, but Haim was as quiet as a mouse, even though he was carrying a heavy bag. I could not believe what was inside;

gold, precious stones, bracelets, and earrings! He said I had to keep them here, in my room, hidden where no one could find them. He said that the Red Army were starting to search all the Jewish houses and businesses, and that if they found anything of value, he would be accused of being a collaborator and shot. I was so shocked that of course I said yes, but where to hide this bag? The chimney was still open, but because we were saving money, there had been no fire in the grate for as long as I could remember. Haim helped me stuff the bag up there, but I kept my own box of gold close by, in its usual place. I could not bear to be parted from it. Haim kissed me before he climbed back down the pergola. He kissed me!

Quite what will happen now, I do not know.

Goodnight.

Nino

***

A garden on the outskirts of Zugdidi greets us with deep banks of greenery and shade echoing with Mingrelian laughter and song. Flowers and fruit are abundant bedfellows, and as we pass through it into the cool, fan-washed, interior of the house, I feel, for the first time, since my arrival in Georgia, completely safe.

This beautiful peaceful place belonged to a family of academic women in Zugdidi, the elegant capital of Mingrelia, and home to generations of Georgian royalty. Their house was full of white cool spaces, elegant dark furniture, and floors so wide and polished, I wanted to lie down and press my cheek to their soft wisdom. Artists, social misfits, and the persecuted have always been welcome in this house. It was a tradition started by their father, who invited any ragamuffin – Georgian or otherwise – to stay. They were fed, cared for, and given space to create, heal, and grow. This generous practice continued after his death under the care-taking eye of his wife, and has since been upheld by his daughters, who are all professional women in their own right. A teacher, a musicologist, a lawyer; none of them married, none of them are mothers, nor burdened by constant compromise, or confused about their purpose in life. I was struck by their grace.

When Nino, Eliso and I arrived, the heat of the day was softened by gentle breezes caught in vines, already full of wrinkled passion fruit, swirling over trellises.

***

Sanctuary

Cool, cool garden.

Dappled sunlight
Gives refuge to
Lush hanging green-red
Grapes and
Kiwi fruit, hard and bitter, wait on the vine.

Apple-peaches
Plump, starflower topped, fill
My mouth, seek corners with her nectar
Which flows through to my deep inside.

Connects me to this land.

Nana fills
With glistening blue-print life
My cupped hands.

I drink.

Her kind eyes scrunch and her garden
Sighs.

***

We crept into the back parlour, where a dark-haired child slept under a sheet. Instinctively, our voices dropped to whispers. The hushed plosives of the Georgian language lulled me into the quiet spaces of the darkened room. I wished only to rest, close my eyes and soak up the soft sounds these women made. Listening to them, I caught their eyes, and, despite having no shared language between us, I sensed they knew my story already. Somehow, it didn't matter. There was a union here, a trust, and a connection. I felt my eyes prick with tears, and relief surged through my body. For the first time in a long time, I found myself wishing I spoke more than a few halting words of this impossible tongue. I wanted to hear their stories for myself.

The woman moving around the kitchen had to be their mother, Nana. Her hands were gnarled but deft as she stirred a simmering pot of sweet *pelamushi*. The honey-sharp smell of red grape juice mingled with the green breezes from outside, as she coaxed the stove-top concoction through its transformation into a solid pink blancmange-like dessert for later. I could see her watching me from the corner of her eye, her skin crinkling either with patient curiosity, or the heat. I wished for a moment alone with her, so we could look at one another squarely.

The meal was not intended to be a *supra* until it was made into one by the arrival of Mr Pulikarpe Khubulava. This 91-year-old played the *chonguri*, Georgia's unique, long-necked, five-stringed, wooden member of the lute family. The sprightly old man was famous for the scandal of having had not one, but three wives, two of whom were still alive, earning him the accolade of '*real* lover of women'. He was a music and folklore expert, and had taught many all-male choirs through generations of oppression by the various invaders of Georgia. Many songs which are now all but lost live on precariously in his memory alone, and have a delightful tendency to trip unexpectedly from his tongue. He spoke, in a voice pregnant with memory, its timbre pure in its discordance, of the distress and pain he felt at not qualifying for a certificate of validation from the head of the Folklore Centre in Tbilisi. The songs his choirs sang – so they said – whilst worthy of study and reference, were not worthy of official recognition. I had heard similar stories from other provincial choirs all over Georgia. This academic indifference not only punctures pride and endangers the country's cultural heritage, it also has a terrible knock-on effect on the salaries these venerable folklorists can command.

Their choirs can no longer travel abroad and teach their repertoires outside the country. When these songs die with the memories containing them, they will be gone forever.

***

Pulikarpe Khubulava

He drives himself
91 years old
To this house.

Sits, thin legs
Broad shouldered still
Weeps, drinks sweet red wine.

He
Sings the notes
Missing for generations, whilst Nino
Pen poised, toes curled, ears pricked
Asks hard questions.

Unifying romantic notions unravel.

"Who will sing my final song?" he asks right back at her.

"Three egoists took my funeral lament with them when they died
Refused to teach me those precious notes."
"How will my soul rest now?"

He weeps, drinks deep red wine
As the women sit, silent.

***

Throughout the evening meal, between conversations about the enormous original paintings on the walls and songs accompanied by the *chonguri*, the dark-haired child watched his mysterious aunts. The old man caught sight of him, and soon had him tending to his every need, slipping chicken and bread, salad, wine, water, dark meat, this, that, the other onto his plate or into his glass, conducted by an eyebrow or a flick of the finger. The wine-jug dwarfed the child, but with great precision, love, and some finesse, he poured the crimson liquid ever-so-carefully into the old man's crystal glass. The only sound throughout the entire delicate process was a single soft chink of crystal on crystal followed by a slight inward breath from one of his aunts. The boy-child in a house full of incredible women sat, gazing with utter adoration, at the one man in the room.

***

My Mysterious Aunts

My mysterious aunts
Always have guests when I am here.

They arrive quite late
On hot summer nights
And ask for a
"Cupp-a-o-tea"
Often, they bring their own blue and white cups
Huge and delicate and
Dig deep into over-sized bags
Root for "sweetandhers" and "earlgay"
Say "No, thank-you" to our black bitter chai.

My mysterious aunts sit
Drink petal-soft
Scented wine for
Hours with grandfathers who ask
Me to pour
Crimson cordial into
Tall, crystal, glasses.

My mysterious aunts

Sing me songs in

The ancient tongues of my

Ancestors

That soothe and ease my eyes

Tired from picking

The red-sour berries

Now turned to jam.

My mysterious aunts

Move without sound towards the dawn, and

When their voices drop to soft lullaby-whispers

I can finally hear the nightingales

Sing.

***

Pulikarpe died in the autumn of 2014, having reached his 92nd year. There was no one left alive who remembered the ancient Mingrelian funeral lament that was so important to him.

12: Five Unexpected Apples in My Bag.

My phone rings. Its echo rebounds through the cavernous spaces of Sameba Cathedral, and because I like the way the tone mutates as it bounces off the enormous columns, I let it ring. I am standing, hands on hips, chewing the fat with Saint Nino. Ramaz watches me from a respectful distance. She likes this. She is used to women nattering with her, I can tell. She perches effortlessly on a flesh-coloured dappled marble ledge in her simple wooden frame. An inlay, pounded by silversmiths, depicts events from her life, and is embedded with jewels designed to mirror her beauty. The same artisans have given her a halo so substantial it looks like a silver pillow, undulating with energy from around her holy head. Nino's hair flows from behind each ear, the scraggy brown ends sitting on her collarbone which is covered in a white swoop of scarf. The story goes that Nino cut her hair short to bind grape vines together to make a cross. Nino holds that very same cross high in this picture, and I am drawn, inexorably and inevitably, towards it. Touching the frame, I look up, past the red prayer book she holds across her left breast, and beyond the blue silk of her dress, into her eyes. My shallow breath catches as I ask for her help. "Nino, protect me at this Tea Party." As my words fade away, so my breath slows and my heart calms. I bow and touch my forehead to the cool glass. I feel the prick of tears.

***

August 3rd 1920

Dear Diary,

Grand-papa is so very angry that he and Grand-Mama have left to go and live with my aunt in Zugdidi. Papa rages around the house, and there are more and more soldiers here every day. Alexei has been promoted, and he and Papa spend long hours shut up in the front parlour. My poor Mother cries all the time, and Keti is stick-thin. I work in the house now. My dreams of going to Vienna have all but disappeared and Haim stays away from me. Yesterday, there was a tiny chunk of gold in the garden. I saw it from my window in the moonlight and collected it this morning. Haim's house is shuttered up. I miss the early morning thwacking sound as he beats the carpets. Sometimes I hear scuffling whispers from inside the walls, but Papa says that they have fled to the mountains.

"Good riddance!" he said. Late summer roses bloom around my window, but my head still aches.

Goodnight.

Nino

***

The second afternoon in Zugdidi, Eliso, Nino and I went to hear a choir of Abkhazian refugee women sing. The heat left ripples like snail trails across the pavements. I was glad for the grey and white air-conditioned walls of the art gallery where the concert was being held. We were late and they were waiting. Wearing blue velvet dresses and open-toed sandals, their nervous smiles flashed broken and missing teeth smattered with gold. I looked at their faces and my heart jumped a little in my chest. I hadn't realised how important this performance was to them.

During Soviet times, the women were considered the best choir in the region. Nino had set them a challenge to perform, for me, an English visitor. She wanted them to sing songs that actually belonged to them, to the culture that connected them to their roots, rather than from the state-sanctioned lists. By so doing, they would be finally breaking the strangle-hold of a propaganda machine with its origins in Stalin's time, a time when territorial and cultural integrity were resolutely ignored. Despite the air of grim disillusion the women wore, this performance would be ground-breaking. It would be the first time they had sung, publicly at least, songs from their homeland.

Nino whispered to me as we waited for the TV in the corner to be turned off. "These women, they have lost all their confidence. You know they did not get their certificate from the Folklore Centre." Her eyes widened in outrage. "What do they have to lose? Why not let them sing their own songs for once?" She shrugged characteristically, knitted her fingers together and rested them, resolutely under her bosom. The women in blue waited nervously for her nod to begin. I held my breath.

Discordant harmonies that both soothed and grated filled the room. With every song they completed, the women relaxed and grew in confidence. They took us on a journey over the lakes and forested hills of their disputed homeland, a territory of abandoned hotels, young women in uniform, and rusting piers jutting into the warm waters of the Black Sea.

We travelled through traditional love songs, raucous shanties complete with suggestive hand gestures and innuendo, a brand new composition set to a poem written by a local woman, and then to the dizzying heights of a soul-soaring melody calling for Jesus and the Nightingale to join together and work as one to save us all. As I watched their eyes and their bodies, I saw, set against the white backdrop of the gallery, the colours of their lives shadow them, swaddle them. Shimmering auras of blue, gold, and yellows danced amid the grey-black-rancid-green memories that threatened to drown them. When the singing finally stopped, the air was charged as though an electric storm had passed overhead.

The ghosts the Abkhazian women had conjured kept us company as the women from the choir walked with us the few blocks to Mzisadari's café. It was a shabby place full of working men and cigarette smoke. Huge overhead fans tried, but failed, to keep the air from becoming putrid. We sat at the back, at a long table piled with misshapen apples, melon slices, and *chvishtari*, baked cornbread with cheese. With no performance to distract us, the focus now fell solely on the ritual of the *supra*. One toast followed another, the first to God as usual, the second to the land, the third to friendship, the fourth to sons now lost, and the fifth to the 'good girls' - *kargi gogoa* - daughters, who watch us from the shadows, their dark eyes cast downwards whenever they thought I was looking. It was time to drink, to sing, and to eat. I nibbled, hoping I was managing to disguise the fact that I was avoiding most of the food. Rich with cheese, the *khachapuri* would have me doubled over with stomach ache, and the strong dark meat in walnut sauce would herald in hours of heartburn. I compensated with lots of salad and fruit, and breathed a sigh of relief when the toasts slowed and the singing started. It was swiftly followed by dancing. As the women started to spin and twirl, like swans in a state of ecstatic release, I too was able to escape the confinement of the table, of my conscious self, and release my own ghosts. Poverty, betrayal, grief, loss, widowhood, distrust, disappointment, and pain were replaced by joy in companionship, connection through song, determination in friendship, and freedom in dance. Just for one moment, one twirling, swirling, joyful moment, I was part of that.

As early as I could without causing offence, I prepared to leave. I hefted my rucksack onto my shoulder, frowning at its unexpected weight. Nino, Eliso, and I walked together, away from the five women who stood on the pavement, smiling, and waving us goodbye. Later, safe back in my room, I looked in my bag and found five apples nestled in amongst the flotsam of my life. Yellowing-bruised, dark-spotted, dull-misshapen, over-ripe red apples bumped around between lipstick, diary, keys, and purse, blossom scenting them with harvest-time memories.

Apples, it seemed, were like guests: gifts from God.

***

Five Unexpected Apples in my Bag

One

You, who say you have never worked
But make a small living from song
Release the bitter pulp of societal scorn
That hangs you low on the gnarled branch of disappointment
Make a balm for the passion that burns in your soul.

Two

Your head need not now dip and bow
The weight of swollen water and gorged promises
Need not keep limbs and will from grace
To stifle childhood rhymes –
Feel now your spirit, strengthen your bough and your song.

Three

Grief claims you
There is no more sun
Tears linger, swell, pool, gush, invade, serenade
The others, who cannot see through this darkness, instead
Pour wine into your glass, pray for your release.

Four

You, flit from branch to branch taking berries
Peg the washing out. Chirruping, you take
Thorny gossip, sunshine sheet whip it
Fold it, knead it, bake it –
Your song lights the hearth.

Five

And now, bitter-sweet you. So long you have been at the top of the tree
Giving shelter, throwing sprigs westward
Back home. Never quite here, never quite there
Your inquisitive fronds seek new silks and dawns
Deepen your roots. Stay still. It will come.

13: Coprolite

St Nino seems to smile as I step outside into the sunshine to answer my phone. It is my friend. I suspect he is a spy. My suspicion is based on a light-hearted conversation earlier in the day when he said, "Let's meet in the main square of the old town. We can go to the café I wrote to you about. It was swept for bugs this morning. It's had the all clear."

"Blimey," I thought. "Is my phone bugged too?"

I was to sit at an outside table and wait for him. He would be exactly one hour.

***

November 18th 1920

Oh diary, what will become of us? Papa has left with Alexis to go to Russia to command part of the Red Army, and Keti has come home. She has shut herself up in her old room, and I hear nothing from her day after day. The remains of the summer roses cling to the crumbling stonework, and I dare not look to check if Haim's bag full of gold is still there. I have buried my own box in the garden, by the back wall. What if the soldiers return and find it? What will they do to me?

The night is the hardest time to feel so alone.

Nino

***

Nino wanted to take me to a region in Samegrelo where a particularly fascinating rite, the Chvenieroba Festival first originated. So, as the first heat waves undulated across the Zugdidi road, the three of us, driven by a taxi recommended by our hosts, waved our friends goodbye and set off to Martvili Monastery, a three-hour drive away. I was keen to visit places where the stories of women have been ignored, especially in light of some reading I have been doing about how high the percentage of sex-selective abortions is here in Georgia. I was also still digesting the Patriarch's recent advice to families who are overrun with children: If they cannot feed their fourth or fifth child, then those children should be given to the church.

That same reading material – a wedge of printed A4 paper – fluttered in my hands, tugged at by open-window breezes. It soaked up bright sunlight which made it difficult to read. Words about St. Andrew meandered and bumped around the pages in synchronicity with the road beneath us. *First century ... St. Andrew, one of the first apostles ... travelled to Georgia ... an end to the ancient ritual of sacrificing a baby ... one a year, every year ... appease the ancient gods.* The car ground and chuntered along pot-holed roads. I gripped, with one hand, the rust-eaten door frame, whilst with the other, I held the crumpled paper as flat as I could in an attempt to read a paragraph about an oak tree at the site of the monastery. It had originally housed a cast copper cage in human form, ready to receive the child sacrifice.

A particularly violent swerve jolted me fully into the horror of my imagination, and in the space inside my skull I heard, rather than saw, a group of men singing. I thought about the many Georgian songs that connect with the ritual of childbirth, and I suddenly understood that they are also sung to protect against evil energies. A *batonebo*, a woman's healing song, floated into my head. I turned my face to the sun. There was change in atmosphere – something in the light played over my eyelids perhaps – so I opened my eyes and watched from the window as we approached the Chanistskali River. We crossed the bridge at speed, the driver challenged the hot metal sheets that lay loosely across rotting wooden beams. The flat rusting panels reared up in protest.

***

Severed Exhaust

Unstable, hot metal sheets

Swaddle Chanistskali bridge

Rivets tear at river's bend as we

All sat up and keen to arrive

Push forward over sheer drop cracks of space beneath

Where

Broken water rumples and cocoons tumble stones from

Distant cousin mountain-tops.

Egg-pebbles skittle as boys who

Brown from acres of sky, haunch, squint, push hard against echoing white light

Pluck up stones

Lob them.

Our car, already lacking suspension

Passes, at some speed towards the far side when the

Rear-end arches to meet the vicious scalpel cut that

Slices, just under me, the exhaust

Clean

Off.

***

The driver picked up the back end of the exhaust from the ruined tarmac and placed it in the boot with a scowl. When the engine rumbled back to life, the car sounded like it belonged on a Formula One race track, and the exhaust fumes billowed inside so that, even with the windows wide open, my stomach lurched and my hands trembled. The driver assured me with a wave of his hand that it was not dangerous. As the roads become narrower, and the roar from the engine ever louder, I insisted, in increasingly anxious tones, that we turn around and return to Zugdidi. Curiosity about ancient rituals at a monastery was not enough to risk my life. Eliso and Nino exchanged glances, and we stopped at the very next garage to try to get the missing exhaust piece welded back on. This happened pretty quickly – the stopping at least, if not the welding. In answer to the call of nature, Eliso and I, still pale and shaky, set off to find the facilities.

Imagine a lean-to. Imagine a lean-to with an ill-fitting slatted door, painted with a cross like a plague house. Imagine this lean-to with its ill-fitting, plague-house, slatted door perched on a concrete block with a hole punched through the middle of it. Imagine the concrete block perched over a pit. Imagine heat, heat combined with an unimaginable smell. Now imagine being inside the lean-to, squatting, having taken a huge breath before you go in, and hoping against hope you have enough air in your lungs to last you last you the time it takes to finish. I imagine it all in an instant. Even though I have been holding my bladder for the last hour, there is no way I am going in there.

***

Lean – to

Ramshackle shack
Holy door swings
On rusting crooked hinges.

My friend
Braver than I
Enters.

Frown of concentration lines her face and
Trying not to breathe more than once
Like a swimmer deep diving she
Gulps air, rushes in
And
Squats
Quick, quick!

I pee round the back
The gaping hole
Yawning chasm
Of shit
Stares at me from
Underneath the
Crumbling concrete
Block and, distracted, I am
Stung by a nettle that
Lurks there.

***

We continued past more mediaeval-style toilets, and moved onto smoother surfaces as we travel towards Martvili. The road was a smooth and broad legacy of Mikheil Saakashvili, the pro-European President who embraced western ideals in return for infrastructure investment. But still, the chickens and cows wandered over it at will.

***

The Land Beneath

Thank you, Misha
For the new road to Martvili.

Past travellers speak of attacking, rutting, gouging terrain. Now
This scold's bridle muffles land of
Bubbling streams, cracked hazelnut groves, skeletal corn fields and
Abandoned ancient cobbled stones that watch, side
Lined as salient ornate filigree balconies, bridges from the past
Bristle with resentment.

Underneath, Misha
Patriarchal land, scattered with golden fleece promises
Calls the beasts from wooded places
And they come, one and all.

Cows, ducks, goats, cocks, chicks, dogs, horses, pigs, bears, wolves.
They are set on
Reclaiming the old road and, oblivious to your ideology, Misha,
they will beat and tear
With brooms and chairs and nettles and with righteous anger
This new road down.

They do not care for your future, Misha
The beasts of the land return
Reclaim the teeming earth.

14: Nino Chooses White Floating Trousers

I wait for my friend, the spy, in the Tbilisi old town main square cafe in anticipation. The meaty smell of khinkhali dumplings fills the air, and I try not to think about the last time I was here. I swallow nervously. I sense echoes of David's place in my past, and my skin crawls. Sweat trickles down my back. A combination of heat and nerves keep me in a state resembling exhaustion. I glance at my watch, and realise that in just four hours time I will be addressing a room full of dignitaries, journalists, artists, and activists.

Nino's diary sits innocently on the table. At last, I can read it without having to hide anything. I am already angry with Alexis, and wonder at his ruthlessness. I fret for Keti, hidden in her room. As for Haim and Nino's love story, my heart pounds every time I think about it. I glance up. A man in a dark suit, dark sunglasses, and a broad smile approaches me.

"Leah!" he cries, and we hug as if we have known each other for years. It is the first time I have met him in the flesh, although we have been corresponding about Georgia and her culture and politics for years. "What's this?" he asks, as he settles himself opposite and points to the diary. His eyes twinkle as I tell him the tale. "Ah yes, I know this house on Erekle Street." He taps the side of his nose, and winks. A hovering waiter delivers two tall, iced lemonades I don't remember ordering.

***

January 6ᵗʰ 1921

Grand-Papa and Grand-Mama have come home now. Grand-Papa wound up the gramophone and built the fire up so hot and raging, I was frightened the chimney would set on fire. We all sat in the front parlour, and talked about what was happening on the streets of Tbilisi, and what would become of us. Then, Grand-Papa looked at me and said, 'Do you still wear the chain of gold with the golden key around your neck?' Mother's head snapped towards me. Grand-Papa nodded to Grand-Mama, and she went to the closed door to answer a gentle knocking. Haim stood on the other side. His face was drawn and tired. I could not help myself, I flew at him, right into his arms, and he wrapped them around me and held me. He smelt of mountainside, rivers, pebbles, and snow. 'Do you have the key?' he asked. I suddenly understood everything. The gold! We were going to use the gold to help ourselves stay Independent. Mother moved towards me, but Grand-Mama stopped her. I took the key off the chain and handed it to Haim. 'No,' he said. 'I don't want your little box of gold, that's yours.' He nodded to Grand-Papa, who went with him to my room to get the bag of precious things hidden in my chimney. As I brushed past Mother, she caught hold of my wrist, and twisted the bare flesh there. Then she slapped me across the face.

I don't understand what I have done wrong. What have I done wrong? I can hear Mother screaming and shouting at Grand-Mama, and the sound of breaking glass. Keti crept into my room and caught me playing with the golden key. Her eyes were haunted in the candle light. 'They are coming for us,' she said. 'They are coming for us.'

Dear God, keep us safe in these mad times.

Nino

***

Martvili Monastery has an enticing serenity about it. Everything is quiet. It is as if all the noise has been absorbed into the blond stone blocks and soft candle wax. We were dropped off by our driver next to a building nestled in a garden overgrown with trees and pomegranate vines. He said he had a cousin in town (or was it an uncle?) with a welding kit. The stairs to the monastery were well-worn, and the perfume of eucalyptus, released from cherished tree-lined thoroughfares, drew us ever upwards. At the top, Father Andrew, who seemed to have been waiting, greeted us warmly, grasped both my hands in his, and pulled them towards the wooden beads and cross that lay over his simple black vestments. Nino explained to him that even though I had pale skin and red hair, I was actually spiritually Georgian, having been baptised into the Orthodox Faith at Mtskhela two summers before. His eyes crinkled and shone as he took us into the church for our own special tour.

***

Nino Chooses White Floating Trousers

Father Andrew has
Kind smiling eyes in a
Brown walnut face and
Spends time
Telling me about Saint Andrew
And all his good deeds.

He calls me Nino
My baptism name.

I unnerve him
In my earnestness.

I think, mistakenly that
My spirit is soothed and
As divisions open in my
Soul.

My white floating trousers
Offend darting, covered women
Who brush, with twigs, and pick with bitten fingernails
The wax from tiny, handmade candles, that drips
Foetid liquefying mounds of prayer.

So

One darts forward and ties, around my hips
A blue sarong, the colour of my eyes.

My sex now covered I can confess
I craved, for an instant, the anonymity of these
Walls.

Should I immerse, plunge?
Should I leave behind the hot fire of my joyful defiant life?
Should I enter the cool nunnery of obedience?

My throat constricts.

I hand back Mary's shawl
And choose white floating trousers.

***

The day I chose to be baptised was the day before I was due to fly home, in summer 2011. The weather was about to change; I could smell the rain coming. David drove, at speed because we were late, to a church nestling in a grove of cedars. I was already angry. Being late for something so important, together with being rejected the night before when David had refused to make love to me, made me feel even more confused. We were late because he had been filming for one of his documentaries. The rest of the choir were already there, as was Father Andria, the priest who was to become my spiritual father. They were all waiting. Sitting on hand-hewn benches, we talked about God and the power of love. What I said seemed to satisfy the black-frocked priest, and so after a little time had passed, he nodded sanguinely, assured and hopeful about his latest convert. We all made our way down to the river.

The entrance was gated, locked, and guarded. There was an electricity station at the side of the river, and no one could enter. The choir smiled smugly, and there was a lot of gesticulation going on. I was disappointed and surprised at my lack of nonchalance. I was curious to know what it felt like to be baptised in the river, having no memory of my infant baptism into the Church of England. Making such a public commitment to David's religion would make things easier for us later when we got married. Father Andria spoke to the guard who, shaking his head and pursing his lips, refused to let us through the gate. I could see that things were going to get more interesting when the priest started to talk into his mobile. He passed the phone to the guard, who listened for a few seconds, then started to nod enthusiastically. He opened the gate and shouted blessings at us as we passed through. The boys from the choir claimed that Father Andria had a direct line to the patriarch, who had, with one word, ensured that the gate was opened.

We drove down the track to the river where, after I had changed into a full length black skirt, black blouse and covered my head entirely with a soft cream head-scarf, stepped into the freezing water. My soon-to-be godfather and the priest were waiting for me. There was no doubting that the total immersion, the sacred oil, the ritual of chant, and the intention in that space and that time was pregnant with a sense of honour and meaning. There was also no doubt that the natural and complete expressions of love shown afterwards at the *supra* were genuine, and there was no doubting the pride everyone felt at the conversion of a foreigner into the fold.

I, however, did not feel any different.

I wanted to make getting married to David easier. He had proposed the previous February. I also figured that if Armageddon were going to come, I would hedge my bets by becoming a member of one of the most fearsome religions in the world. Did I lie to them? Not at the time, no. Did I lie to myself? I don't think so. Am I sorry that I did it now? Yes. But only because of the feelings of disappointment in a community that had welcomed me with such open arms when I was conforming to their expectations, but which had turned their backs on me when I was hurting, and questioning the very essence of their teachings.

In the end, I returned the passport that Father Andria gave me, and along with it, my official status as a member of the Orthodox church, to my godfather with a note. When my time comes, I would like to be buried in a quiet English graveyard, preferably under a shady tree. No keening and highly ritualised toasting for me, thank-you. If anyone wants to scatter wildflower seeds above me, however, I would be most grateful.

15: The Sacrifice

After our meeting at the de-bugged cafe in Tbilisi's old town, I am now in the spy's car. I luxuriate in the air conditioning, and joke about the Tea Party. He can tell I am nervous.

"Don't worry," he says, "I will be there. Nothing bad will happen." A big red button on the dashboard starts to blink.

"Do you need fuel?" I ask.

"Nope," he laughs loudly, "That's the ejector seat."

***

February 15th 1921

The Red Army has invaded Tbilisi. All is hell here now. Papa is back. I saw him in his uniform. He came to inform Mother that the house would be used as a base for his officers, and that she needed to prepare everything that was necessary. I hid behind the curtains and prayed he would not see me. Haim's house was quiet and still as usual, even though I know he is there, working through the dead hours of the night, doing God only knows what.

Nino

***

I had had enough of Martvili monastery, and I could tell Eliso had too, but our driver was not answering his phone. To kill time, I retrieved the crumpled ethnographic study about child sacrifices in pre-Christian Georgian society from my bag. The sacrifices had been carried out on this very spot, in Martvili.

"How did they do it, Nino?" I asked. She shrugged, and dialled the number of a friend who would know. With one shoulder hunched, cradling her mobile phone, she talked to a friend at the conservatoire in Tbilisi. I watched her face transform from its usual, mildly inquisitive expression to one of outright horror.

"Ara, ara, ho, ho," she muttered - no, no, yes, yes - glancing towards me. I could tell she was weighing up just how much of this new information she wanted to share.

"Eliso," I asked, suddenly worried, hoping for a translation of the stream of Georgian buzzing just out of earshot, "What is she saying?" Before Eliso could answer me, Nino scurried up towards the monastery, her legs hardly keeping up with her intention, and disappeared behind the church. "Find out what's going on, and then tell me!" I said breathlessly to Eliso as we snatched up our bags and followed.

By the time I arrived, panting, on the other side of the church, Nino and Eliso were deep in conversation. There was much arm flapping, hands covering horrified mouths, and cheeks red with shock being cradled by palms, aghast with too much detail. Nino refused to make eye contact with me as Eliso shared the information that had upset her so much. "The priests took their chosen child, and it was burnt alive in a copper cage hung from an oak tree. The cage was shaped either like a man or an eagle – no-one is quite sure. The only way into the cage was through the mouth. The child was always alive."

It was my own hands, this time, that flew involuntarily to my horrified mouth, and the prick of salt tears burned cheeks that had been dried by the acrid heat. Was it the fact that we were all mothers that made this information hit so hard, or was it that we were right in the very same place where these crimes had been committed? Instead of just words on paper, one more atrocity in the grim roll-call of atrocities that make up our history, this felt real and immediate, as though time had collapsed in on itself and the sacrifices happened just yesterday. I felt a stoicism come over me.

"Where is the oak tree?" I asked, then continued without waiting for an answer, "Are there any oak trees here?" I wanted to touch the gnarled bark. I wanted to lay my hands on the land that held the screams of these children in order to try and understand, perhaps to try and heal it. Silently, grimly, we wandered the grounds, searching for an oak tree but found none. Despite the heat, I was cold. I wanted to leave and never return. Nino's phone rang. The driver had returned.

Bumping in the back seat of the car, back through grape-filled fields, bathed in late-summer light towards Zugdidi, I scoured the roadsides and horizons for the oak trees that had come to symbolise such fear in pre-Christian Georgia, but their tell-tale silhouettes were nowhere in sight. I re-ran the conversations I had had with Nino about this ancient ritual over and over in my mind. Oblivious to the general car chatter, to the backfiring exhaust, and to the darkening, end of day sky, my eyes grew heavy. I felt myself slipping into that in-between place where the veil between the past and present, the living and the dead is so thin it's easy to slip into another world.

***

They came on Saturday. The priests of the idol, with their robes and their chanting. And they waited, like hovering eagles. And they held out their clawed hands, for my token.

My white pebble was covered in ochre dots, one for each member of my family. They spiralled into the centre, where the last dot, golden like the sun, flashed as it went, into a basket woven from reeds by the river.

My river.

The river where I sang to my unborn son every day. Where I had sung to the moon each night, and watched my belly grow until he came to me, my boy.

"How many?" my son's father asked the priests, eyes cast down. Early spring daisies littered our front garden and, as my boy sat on one hip, I felt the other child within me stir. My heart tightened with their reply.

"Sami, three tokens."

"It will be an honour if we are chosen," my husband murmured and scuffed with his foot at a stick that snapped the head from one of the flowers.

Watching the priests leave, I felt the heat of my child's face against my shoulder. He had been unwell. A spring fever. The feverfew and lavender had only soothed, not cured. His skin burned and I saw tiny red flowers start to appear on his cheeks. His tongue was swollen, the colour of raspberries. I hurried inside. The spirits needed to be welcomed. Once inside the room, I covered the walls with red cloth, and sang to him as he lay restless and hot in my arms.

Lullaby, lullaby,

Violets opened roses, petals lullaby,

I'll meet Batonebi's aunt with pleasure, lullaby,

I'll see her in as a godsend guest, lullaby,

With a carpet on the floor, lullaby.

As he drifted in and out of sleep, I took, from my private place, the dagger. I tied the five red stones I had taken from the river to the handle, and hung it on the wall opposite his bed. I sang as I did it; 'Lullaby, Lullaby.' Later that day, my husband came back. Shaking his head, he placed my token on the red cloth I had covered in flowers and sweet wine. My boy had been chosen.

Guests started to arrive before I was ready for them. Some bought eggs, some flour, some dried fruit, but they all bought wine, and they all looked at me with horror in their eyes. Hushed whispers accompanied quiet toasts, and gifts were left by the fireplace. There were dolls made from sticks, beads, and shells. The men started to sing, long low baleful sounds that cut through the night air, drifting up to the sacred space where chqondidi, the Oak Tree, and the priests were waiting.

My boy's fever broke in the early hours as the cock crowed. The red Sunday dawn brought with it the box with wheels. My son had to go, swaddled, in that box, through the village, up to the sacred place. I don't remember who made the box. I think it was the boy's father. I felt he had done so with a heavy heart. Watching my son sleeping peacefully in the early morning light, I knew I had to stop this terrible thing from happening. I had to do something, something to save him.

I had heard of a man, a man far away, who had cut down the old oak with an axe that had glinted so brightly in the sunlight that the people had been blinded by it. I begged and begged my husband to help me, to save our boy. I begged him to find this saviour. But he beat me and I fell on the hard stone floor. Curling around my belly as he kicked me over and again, I knew all was lost.

I don't remember much else, only the bitter taste of the tincture I had given my boy to help him pass over. He, before he went, seemingly asleep, on the cart, opened his eyes. I kissed his nose. "Deda," he whispered. I had swaddled him tight.

I followed the cart to the sacred place. As the moon broke from behind the midnight clouds, I watched the priests put him in the cage.

The oak groaned.

I smelt the burning of his flesh. The oak sighed.

I heard him scream. The oak swayed.

And the eagles circled.

***

Sacrifice the Children to the Chqondidi.

Moonshine razor rivet screams choke on copper smoke
That hide
For an instant, this man-beast-bird
Gibbet that hangs, cradles
Low plucked fruit. My out of season child
That
Pulsed his way into this idol world.

Here, chanting men will never
Feel the tug of lips on breast, or smell the sweet scent
Of hair, like white daisies outside our door.

Did they notice his bow-mouth tremble?
Did the singe-blond flop of his baby curls scorch their souls
As they lit the fire beneath?

Acrid tears tear my eyes as I will my
Salt slit womb to poison the life
Within.

16: Corpses

"Where to?" asks the spy.

"Zakariadze Street." I reply.

"Ah yes. Your visit to the Women's Fund." he says.

"How on earth…?" I am confused. How did he know?

"You might have mentioned it," he interrupts, "in one of your emails."

I frown. I cannot remember if I mentioned it or not. The silence that grows between us is comfortable, however, as he navigates the pot-holed roads, and avoids skewed cars, parked precariously across pavements.

"I have tried to tell my neighbour about this organisation you are visiting." he says. The tick-tock of the indicator holds the moment.

"Why?" I ask.

"I hear her most nights, crying," he tells me, not meeting my eye. "In fact I heard her this morning, crying. She had taken another beating from that bastard who calls himself her husband." His knuckles whiten as he grips the steering wheel, and I can see his jaw clench.

"Oh dear God," I say, slumping in my seat, "Where are the police in all this? When David threatened me, the UK police were right on it. It stopped."

"You know they don't care, Leah," he says, finally looking at me, a sardonic smile crossing his lips. "It's seen as a private matter. An officer will visit, sure, but more often than not, he will end up drinking with the bastard abusers." The spy's thin smile gives way to fury, and his voice lowers. "Do you know about the increase in hate crime against women here?" I shake my head. "There was a case, last week, all hushed up, of a woman who was beaten up, and left for dead in her own flat. The flat was set on fire and she was left to burn." I nod. I had heard about this. The woman had been vociferous about women's rights, and the rights of the LGBTQ community in Tbilisi.

"My friend was friends with the woman at the university who was shot by her husband," I say. "This is why I want to visit the Women's Fund. I want to find out more."

"They won't be able to help much," he says, the tick-tock of the indicator once more adding anticipation to his words. "Their funding has just been cut."

***

Femicide

Have you ever had a death threat?

I have. Seriously.

Have you ever told people about the death threat only to be greeted with platitudes of, "Oh he would never do that, he may say he would … it but he would never do it."

I have. Seriously.

Have you ever been threatened by his friends, been told you were a liar, you were attention-seeking or that these things were a private matter, and not to be spoken about publicly?

Have you been told that you, "Did it to yourself"?

That you were crazy, and ought to be ashamed?

I have. Seriously.

Have you ever had people who are in denial about the toxicity of a society look at you with pity, as you struggle to understand how this has happened to you … to you?

If only, YOU, would shut up.

JUST. SHUT. UP.

I have. Seriously.

The hatred for women is growing.

If you are a woman who happens to be active

If you are a woman who pokes the blind eye

Who paints rainbow colours on the steps of public indifference

If it is you who makes a paper aeroplane out of the letter, hand-delivered to the

Head of your household by the policeman who laughs as he

Reminds you not to show your bruises in public.

Could you fold it please, and from your ninth-floor, post-Soviet, concrete-crumbling apartment

That drips and

Stinks of lies and drink

Let it go, so that I may find it and come and

Release you.

For you, my sister, are lost.

Ashes of good intention drift over the plateau.

Your children are silent now.

The stick he used to beat you with, lies smouldering by the blackened bed.

Where is the key he forced inside you?

Jagged, charred, and now crevice-concealed by a concerned neighbour

Who wiped it clean right after

He turned it against

You

That last time.

Silence does not help; it disempowers everyone.

***

April 5th 1921

Dear God, dear God, Haim is dead. They shot him, right outside the house. Right next to the far wall. I heard the shouting. There were so many men shouting, and doors banging, and glass being broken. Then he was there, outside, and they were beating him, and blood ran from a cut on his forehead. Haim, my own Haim. I saw him. I saw it all. The rose, the climbing rose hid me from view as I looked out of my window, and saw the smoke from the guns before I heard their shots. I saw him slump down hard, heard him thud heavy against our back wall.

I heard, before I saw Alexei, give the order to search the house. 'Find the traitor!' Alexei commanded. A swish of skirt behind me made me catch my breath. Out of the corner of my eye, I saw Mother move quickly past my open door. She must have seen what I had seen. I clamped my hand to my mouth. Do not scream. Do not scream. Papa's voice rang out across the garden, followed by more gunshots, and the sound of running.

Haim's house was being cleansed of what Papa called 'vermin'.

God help me, God help me, God help me.

Nino.

***

In the relative safety of a large swaying coach, Nino, Eliso and I travelled from Zugdidi back to Tbilisi. The only highway between the two regions swept under long tunnels, clung to mountainside valleys, and lined itself with gathering cadaver-corpse cars. During the four-hour journey, window-seat snuff-shows gave a surreal glimpse that made real, the black-and-white words from the Georgian guidebook that rested on my lap.

'The percentage of deaths from car accidents for both Georgians and foreigners is high, with one person injured every hour in a traffic-related accident, while one death occurs every 18 hours. This is according to a study released by the Safe Driving Association, an NGO. The World Health Organisation puts the number of fatalities at 16.8 people per 100,000 people each year.'

***

One death occurs every 18 hours on Georgian roads.

That's quite high.

The only road from Kutaisi
To Tbilisi via Imereti
Undulates, regurgitates river-bed red, pregnant-belly pots.

Pungent ancient soil morphs at
Mountain forest-verge-side into three-footed fug, shrouded black cauldrons
boiling corn.

Multiple wooden cross-squandered lives sit amidst
Rusting car carcasses.

Caught in the eddies of death-trap memories
I catch lamenting
Keening grandmothers, whose crashing hearts ache and connect with
New collisions.

We pass, from the illusory comfort of our air-conditioned coach
Three accidents.

All fatal.

I cross myself
Three times
Just to be sure
As is the custom.

***

The closer we got to Tbilisi the sicker I felt. The granite-grey boulder in my stomach ground against itself. The illusion of safety I had created, deep inside myself, to use as protection whilst exploring the western side of Georgia was crumbling. I could no longer ignore the fact that David must know I was in the country by now. We were heading into Tbilisi that evening to the Rezo Gabriadze Marionette Theatre, to see a quirky, wholly eccentric and eclectic puppetry piece under a quirky, wholly eccentric, wonky clock tower. Getting there meant walking through cobbled Old Town streets, and facing, squarely, memories of happier, love-soaked, arm-entwined times.

17: Ghosts

"Well that was interesting," I say to the spy as I hop back into his car. He looks up from his laptop. He has been catching up on calls and emails while waiting for me to finish my meeting.

"Really? How so?" he asks.

"I felt they were holding something back," I reply, frowning. "But at least they are coming to the Tea Party. They want to highlight domestic violence issues during their five-minute slot, but they mostly talked about not offending anyone." I clench my hands in my lap in frustration. "What is it with this preoccupation with everyone being so bloody nice all the time? How can anyone be nice when talking about rape and femicide?" My knees ache, a sure sign my period is about to arrive. "Shit," I mutter. The spy glances towards me, and before he pulls out into the traffic, he touches my arm.

"It will be alright," he says.

As we pass the steel mesh curves of the Bridge of Peace on the way back to Eliso's flat, the spy turns in his seat to look at me. "Do you fancy another visit to Erekle Street?" he asks. "There is plenty of time." I check my watch. There is not plenty of time but I say yes anyway. He parks directly on Erekle II Square outside the headquarters of The Georgian Dream, the hodge-podge coalition running the country with the single apparent aim of discrediting the former pro-Western, Saakashvili administration. There is a medium-sized protest, consisting largely of older women, going on.

"What is it about?" I ask, staring at the placards as though pure force of will alone could unravel the meaning hidden in the loops and curlicues of the Georgian alphabet. He glances at the banners.

"The way orphans are being treated in orphanages," he replies. He takes my arm, and we walk away from the curious stares, down the cobbled street towards the old house. I glance back and see a police officer approach the car. He turns and stands, resolutely, as if on guard.

The house is unchanged. The gap in the fence is still there, and the window is still open. We move, together, across the rough, uneven ground towards the house. On the warm breeze, I catch the sickly scent of a thousand yellow roses dying on the stem. "I'll wait for you out here," the spy says. As I clamber in through the fence, I hear the strike of a match, and the inhale-exhale of a man content with his cigarette for company.

Once inside, the stairs beckon and I start to climb. Creaks accompany me, and as I lean against the wall to steady myself, I am drawn back in time. I hear hiccupping sobs, pulling me up to the top landing, and a door which swings open at the slightest touch. I sense, rather than see, a bed in the middle of the room. There is a blur of movement around it, hints of body shapes and flashes of black, making me blink hard. I try to focus, but the evening light plays with my mind, and I see the figures begin to shroud the body of a man that lies on the bed. An obelisk of light from the window bathes the figure where it lies, and I see, for a second, the agonised face of a young weeping woman. I watch her reach up and take hold of something that lies against her chest. It is a tiny golden key. I too reach up to touch the key I now wear around my neck. I begin to shake and I miss the moment the room returns to empty. There is only the sound of mice nesting in the rose bushes that have grown over the roof and dropped down and through the blackened chimney.

"Blessed is the Judge of Truth," the spy says to me as I crawl back out through the window.

"What?" I say, patting dust out of my sleeves. He points to some spidery writing scratched into the plaster underneath the window.

"Blessed is the Judge of Truth," he repeats. "It's a Jewish blessing for the dead. Something bad must have happened here."

"Yes," I say. "It did."

***

May 5th 1921

They took Grand-Papa today. They said he was a spy. The cries of women echo through the streets of Tbilisi. No one knows where he has gone. Probably he will be transported to Siberia and the labour camps.

He was here when I left this morning to go to the market, and not here when I got back. Now there is just an empty space where he used to sit, and some charred papers on the floor by the fire.

When will this end?

Nino

***

July 18th 1921

We are poor and I am 17. No one wants to learn how to play the piano anymore, and anyway, the soldiers took all Mother's music. And the gramophone. Keti told us that she found a job as an assistant at the local school, so she could bring in some money, and my fingers burned in shame as I hid my golden key deeper in my clothes. No-one mentions my box or Haim's gold. Grand-Mama looks at me sometimes as if she does not see me, then she turns back to the clothes she is washing and reaches for the lavender water. Now, it is Mother who beats the dust from stranger's carpets on our line, and weeds grow in Haim's garden.

The soldiers said we could send Grand-Papa a parcel every month, so Mother and Grand-Mama are eating less, so they can send him food. I am eating less too, and have taken all my dresses in. I feel like I am diminishing, and I know my eyesight is getting worse. Grand-Mama gave me Grand-Papa's glasses. She said I could use them until they have enough to send the first parcel. Then they must go in with the food. I am careful with them. He will need them wherever he is. We are bartering with our neighbours for food now too. We have so many grapes, but everyone has grapes and wine. We need flour and cheese. We are a family of women, and people look at Mother with suspicion in their eyes. There are very few neighbours left who will help us. I feel so ashamed.

Nino

***

Erekle Street

I remember when
The boy next door
Threw beautiful things into
Our garden.

Things like
Golden rings inscribed with a script so
Delicate that swan-shaped bracelets
Bowed reverent heads and
Turtles, with outstretched limbs and emeralds for eyes
Played hide and seek amongst our rioting passion-fruit vines.

Sometimes, when we
Played archaeologists
We unearthed golden shaped beans
Amongst the wildflowers that stomped
And stormed against the back sunlit wall.

Uneven cobbled streets were our friends
They rang out with
Childish laughter as we rolled our inside-outside bicycle wheels through
Sunshine-shade, through sunshine-shade, towards the river
That called us to her with her song.

Then

They came in the discontented winter and
Took my Grandfather for being a good man. They left
Only charred papers in a burnt-out grate and
Four women whose cracked hands bled and beat
River washed wool to within an inch of its life.

Stones cracked, shutters rotted, balconies crumbled
Mice made homes in windowsill holes
Where once there were silk-spun drapes but now
Wild yellow roses dwell.

My poor mother slaved to feed and believed
Dulce et decorum est
(The old lie)
Non est mortuus
(He is not dead)
Every month she sent
In a brown paper parcel
With 'Sorry' written on the
Inside:

Bread from our oven
Cheese from the neighbours' goats
Meat from the village
Apples from our tree
Socks knitted by guttering candle light and
Handkerchiefs made from curtains
To the punishing frozen north.

The first month
She sent
Shoes, a book of
Poetry and
His reading glasses which, whilst cracked would
Have to suffice.

There was never any reply.

As I peer through the gap in the demolition boards
A rubble of childhood memories gaze back at me and
I see yellow roses wink and riot defiantly
Against the back wall in the
Lengthening shadow of a
Dying sun.

(See endnote)

***

"Can you take me to the statue of Mother Georgia?" I ask. The spy glances at his watch and smiles.

"Are you putting off the inevitable?" he says. I wink at him as I shrug out my answer.

"What can I do?" I say.

He laughs.

***

The last time I was here was in the early hours of a September morning in 2009. David and I walked up to Kartlis Deda, the statue of Mother Georgia. She commands the skyline. With one hand, she grips her great iron sword, crossing it across her body defiantly. With her other, she holds a welcoming bowl of wine skyward. Our walk was accompanied by cicada song, and I felt elated. The heady early morning eucalyptus scent reminded me of my Australian childhood. The path was steep, and I clung to the intermittent railings, until at the top and out of breath, I was able to slow my heartbeat and look out across the city. It was stunning and quiet. The silence was thick with expectation. The heat from David's hands, so close to mine on the railing, made my head spin.

Turning slowly, his little finger brushed mine and as he moved, he held my gaze for what seemed like an eternity. I noticed he was shaking. Then, from below us came the sound of men singing, long and low.

"Let's go," he said.

Making our way down, slowly because of the hazardous pathway, we met the ad hoc choir. They had gathered at an elbow point of the precarious path. We drank deep red wine poured for us from coke bottles, and we toasted to Georgia. David sang with them, intertwining his voice with theirs. The sound swelled and filled the valley. The nighttime stars, increasingly incongruous in the growing morning light, began to fade and I teetered, unsure and dizzy on the steep slope. As we made our way down, the silence between us sparked.

"What will happen if I fall?" I asked.

His reply, as he linked his arm with mine, sealed my fate. "I will catch you."

18: Supra-napped

My dear spy drops me off outside the clean vertical lines of the Public Broadcasting House, its aerials scraping the sky. The sticky heat lies heavy, even as the last of the light of my last day in Tbilisi is dying. My phone rings. It is Eliso. "Come back now," she says, relief and pride evident in her voice. "We are all ready for the Tea Party and waiting for you.' I am amazed, and as I walk towards her high-rise apartment block, I see three taxis waiting for passengers, cakes in boxes, and newly washed teacups. Ramaz sits inside one of the cars playing with his phone. His face lights up as he sees me. I go to open the door but he shakes his head violently, pointing at a dog lounging in the shade beside the car. A tagged ear means she is sterilised and vaccinated, and I see, right next to her, a bowl of water and some flies that buzz around a chunk of meat. She belongs to no-one. She wags her tail at me as I ruffle her ears. Her dugs are bloated and heavy, showing signs of mastitis.

I think about Ava, my beautiful, cushion-eating, piano-leg chewing, legs-stretched-out-behind-her, chestnut brown-eyed Labrador-collie cross, who waits for me at home. Like this swollen, abandoned creature, she is Georgian too, and I adore her. Two years ago, she wandered out into the road, and David ran her over. I made him stop the car. I got out and marched back to where she had dragged herself into a ditch. I scooped her up and cradled her. I pleaded with David, who leaned, bemused at all the fuss, on his car, to take me to an English-run D.O.G. shelter in Tbilisi I had heard about. I was going to take her home.

***

Ava

Eight weeks old.
Already nearly blind and
Flea-Ridden
Ticks colonise your ears
Paws, nose, and multiply in the heat
From my breast
As I hold you.
Your heart slows and
From warning, fear-filled, pain-howling
You stretch, yawn, sleep.

I wrap you in my scarf
My body shaking, sobs and fevered tears
Mingle with your hot relieved urine as it trickles
Down my arm, stains my skirt.

Eight minutes after being
Knocked senseless, your beaten, torn, discarded form
Not quite broken
Finds sanctuary in my arms.

***

"I can't believe how easy it will be for this dog to get a visa," David had laughed at me. "Maybe I will throw myself under a car for this love-visa, and live in the UK with you too." The sound of Ramaz knocking at the window from the safe, cool space from inside the taxi jerks me back to the present. He is horrified, gesticulating, bouncing, and shouting at me to move away from the dog. But still, does not get out of the car.

"I'll be 10 minutes," I mouth. He waves and smiles as he leans back, phone in hand, relief showing on his face as I move away from the street dog. My back aches, my womb contracts, and my heart hurts. "Please, body, not yet," I pray, attempting to ward of my impending menstruation with stubborn refusal. "Give me a little more time." My mouth is pressed into a grim line as the lift swings and creaks its way up to Eliso's floor.

The flat is – quite incredibly – calm. Eliso's artful cake-creations nestle in sturdy boxes near the door. A fan, trained on them, whirrs and hums. Moist cream sponge squares soaked in peach juice, and topped with slices of kiwi-fruit in the shape of crescent moons, peek up at me from under rustling, drifting tissue-paper. Cherries suspended in jelly, and whipped cream crafted into seashell cups, adorn heavenly, chocolate-layered, syrup-glazed ovals. They invite finger picking, lifting, eating, but I resist. The various sounds of preparation for a big night out float out of corridor doorways.

"Leah!" Eliso exclaims, almost colliding with me as she comes out of her bedroom, hands stretched around her back, battling with a stubborn zip. "Come on, come on, we must go!" She eyes me up and down, narrows her eyes, pauses. "I will leave you to get ready."

I wash, I pack, I take tablets for the pain, and I pray.

"Please, let everyone behave themselves," I mutter. "Please."

There will be a selection of English tea, including rhubarb, but I know what it is like when Georgians get together. The last thing I need is for my Tea Party to be *supra*-napped.

***

Grand-Mama knocked at my door earlier. Her eyes were dark and she beckoned me to follow her. We went into Papa's stale, angry room. "Sssshhhh!" she hushed me, when I started to ask what was going on. She lit a candle and placed it on the floor. She pushed me into a seat as she began to sing one of our ancient women's songs. She handed me two sticks, and cut some of her hair, which she then used to tie them together to make a cross. Then she cut some of my hair and used that to secure the swags of material and lace in the middle. She impaled the head of the doll, made of a bag stitched together from material taken from curtains in Mama's room, on the cruciform body, and then added layers of veils and beads. As she drew a face with a charcoal stump from the dead fire, the doll came alive under her hands. All the time, she sang, and as the candle flame wavered, she began to move in a circle around the room. I stood up and followed her, mesmerised by her eyes and the light that threw long shadows on the walls. A rumble of thunder from outside broke the spell, and as she shooed me out of the room she pursed her lips and held her finger tight to them, warning me to keep me silent.

Dear diary, if ever I needed the power of our women's magic to help us, it is now.

Nino

***

My first experience of being *supra*-napped was on my first trip to Georgia in September 2009. I had travelled there with three friends from the UK. We had bonded through our love of singing resonant Georgian folk music, and had made a modest name for ourselves in Georgian musical circles. We arrived in Tbilisi at 3 a.m., and all I could think about was a hot shower and my bed. Instead, we were ushered into a vast marble hall with a great table groaning with walnut dishes, cake, and steaming, heady, meaty dumplings. Our host, a short plump woman, who flapped a thick orange towel about gesticulated at us wildly. "Eat! Eat!" she commanded, hiding a gap-toothed smile behind her hand. Despite the humidity and exhaustion, we ate heartily and drank heavily. One toast followed another, and before long, the room started to spin.

When we weren't performing, we spent every waking moment (as well as some decidedly half-awake ones) being plied with vast amount of delicious food, or being ferried at the drop of a hat between sweltering coastlines, rolling hills, and soaring mountains. It was a whirlwind experience that left us feeling kidnapped both by hosts, and by Georgia herself. It didn't matter whether we had already made plans months before to see some amazing sight or another, if our host's friends' cousin's uncle's cabin was free up by Ananuri lake, then we just *had* to go and taste the most delicious *khinkhali* in Georgia! To this day, I do not understand how we survived the journey back from the lake that night. Our hosts were both stoned and drunk, and pungent marijuana smoke wafted thickly into the back seat of the car where we sat, elbow-to-elbow, and petrified.

My first two or three *supras* in Georgia were fascinating. The highly ritualistic toasting, the way the men open up their hearts to express the pride they have for their country, their traditions, their women, their land, is endearing. The banquet is often accompanied by folk songs, and it is inevitably the memory that most visitors to Georgia rave about when they return home. *Supra* is seen as an opportunity to take guests on a journey through the history and culture of the country, accompanied, of course, by *lots* of drinking. Imagine riding a roller-coaster through every terrain and weather condition, accompanied by unrecognisable food, divine wine, and hypnotic song. It travels so fast that your imagination, already overloaded by tales of valour, romance, and majesty, reels, and your sense are jumbled until they are so overwhelmed by it all, that you mistake an extreme emotional experience for love. Imagine all that, and then put *ch'ach'a* into the mix. *Ch'ach'a* is a clear spirit, a little like brandy, vodka, or *grappa*, made from pomace, the leftover bits from the winemaking process. It's incredibly strong, but your hosts are mightily affronted if you don't drink it. After some early grave misadventures, I am afraid I offended several hosts over a number of years.

As my relationship with Georgia deepened into something so much more than a holiday romance, I slowly realised that every *supra* I went to was the same as the last. Mountains of food, made by women who served but did not participate, were left uneaten. Teary-eyed men mumbled into mobile phones, not actually listening to one another at all. At each supra I sat in the corner, a smile frozen on my face as I pretended to drink endless shots of *ch'ach'a*, in the increasingly desperate knowledge that the experience could last for up to six hours.

Alcohol fuels emotions and Georgians are emotional – immediately so. In the beginning, I found this freedom of emotional expression liberating, but I now know that it is a dangerous place to be. It's dangerous because on this roller-coaster ride of emotion there is no stop button, either for your hosts or for yourself. Anyone not used this all-encompassing performance can be left utterly exhausted. By the time I left Georgia for the last time that fateful February in 2012, all I could see in the *supra* was darkness. I didn't want to ride that roller-coaster again.

***

The Ch'ach'a Dance

Eyes cast down, demure hand
Flirts, lofty fingers dapple
Arched eyebrows
Satiated lips.

Elixir breath unseats
Gliding, invisible steps
Contained, restrained, until
Star-shine loosens limbs
And demure masked delusion is breached by
Slamming bitter consumption
Competition
Reprisal.

Moves and countermoves
Twirl, spin, leap, lurch, and bind
Together, in spirit and song
Adoration
Emulation
Emancipation.

Ch'ach'a's misfortune shores up
A dearth of talent in effervescent garb
As camera captures the inkling blink
Of a disappointed smile.

I leave, breathless and exhausted.

19: 'Strong Voices Together' at Tbilisi National Library

STRONG VOICES TOGETHER
A Celebration of the UK & Georgia

The Northern Georgian Society is delighted and honoured to bring you a fusion of Georgian and UK culture at an 'English Tea Party' from 7.45pm, July 2nd 2014, in the Great Hall of Tbilisi's National Library.

The Northern Georgian Society has been bringing Georgian artists to the UK for more than five years. We have also organised school exchanges, hosted art, literary, and musical events in both the UK and Georgia, building bridges between two ancient and strong-minded cultures, with the values of tolerance, inclusion, dignity, integrity, and open-mindedness.

It is in this spirit of inclusion that we bring together artists, writers, free-thinkers, singers, poets, spiritual, political and social leaders from Georgia and the UK, to act as advocates for positive change, coming together to share their work, ideas and visions for the future. Our guests will present their thoughts and feelings about cultural matters linking Georgia and the UK, over fragrant English tea and delicious cake, against the stunning backdrop of the Great Hall of Tbilisi's National Library.

Each segment of the evening will be themed, the first being, 'History & Culture,' the second, 'Women's Voices,' and the third, 'Evolution & Transformation'.

20: You've Made Your Bed.

"Hello, hello!" I say, as I shake hands with the archbishop of the Evangelical Baptist Union of Georgia. We air-kiss, and his eyes crinkle with delight as I embrace his wife.

"How many years is it now since you brought that wonderful Georgian choir to Oxford?" she asks.

My mind blanks. "Too many," I mumble, then, "You look well."

The archbishop rescues me: "Let me introduce you to my dear friend," he twinkles. "He is a professor of English at Oxford." I shake the esteemed gentleman's hand, talking Shakespeare and St Hilda's for a few moments before I am summoned before the TV crew for an interview. My guests from England drift towards the magnificent central display of cakes and teacups, admiring the fronds and flowers Eliso has worked so hard to display.

"Look into the camera, not at the interviewer," Eliso translates, nervously twisting her newly manicured nails into her palms. The girl with the microphone is impossibly young, and impossibly bored. She flicks her wrist watch and yawns. I can see Natia from the corner of my eye, but resist the impulse to excuse myself and cross the room to talk to her. I address the mechanical eye, held an unblinking 20 cm from my face instead.

"The purpose of this event is, of course, to say a huge thank you to the many artists and creative people who have supported the work of the Northern Georgian Society, both here in Georgia and in the UK, over the years," I say, flashing what I hope is a winning smile. "This evening, I hope to encourage a fusion of both cultures, across many different sections of society, giving a voice to those who do not normally receive attention – or indeed recognition – for the work they do." I am on a roll now, not even the supreme boredom of the interviewer, as she examines her manicure, can put me off. "I am particularly excited to have with us this evening an eclectic mix of Georgian artists and activists, who will be sharing with us their stories of what it is like to live in a Georgia dedicated to evolution and transformation."

A flicker of irritation passes over the face of the girl with the microphone. This is not what she wants to hear. She wants to hear me gush about the great traditions of Georgian song and food, its ruby wine, the wonderful tradition of the *supra*, the mountain ranges, and how generous and tolerant the people of Georgia are. Before she can formulate a question to bring me back in line with expectations, I square my jaw. "That's enough!" I snap, and walk away.

"Natia!" I call, crossing the room towards a safer space. Natia is a feminist activist, and she looks like one, with her spiked-up hair, pierced nose, and low-slung jeans. Everything about her screams 'Fuck You!' and I love her for that. She strides across the room, and we embrace.

"Shall I speak in English or Georgian?" she asks. I know the meaning hidden in her seemingly innocent question. If she speaks in Georgian, she risks hostility from her own people, but if she speaks in English, she risks simply losing the majority of her audience. I swallow slowly and, despite the air conditioning, feel a sheen of sweat form on my back.

"Do you want to wait, and gauge it at the time?" I reply. She is sanguine, and her determination gives me courage. But then, she did survive a homophobic attack by tens of thousands of priests.

The Great Hall of the library is full. People have arrived on time, and the men are wearing trousers. I smile triumphantly. Georgians are notoriously late, and it is an uphill battle to get the men to wear anything other than their favourite denims. Important anniversary? Wear jeans. A lovely trip to the theatre? Put your jeans on. Meet the Mayor? Jeans. When I try to explain how rude being late is, and how inappropriate wearing jeans can be, I am greeted with a shrug of the shoulders and a "What can I do?"

So far so good. The choirs are mingling with the officers from the Department of Internal Relations, the founder of the Sun Festival is chatting with the feminist activists, and the academics are giggling (in English) with the Baptist church ministers. Contrasting modern and traditional artwork surrounds the audience, and the atmosphere is electric. By the time I see the spy, he is already watching me with a mild expression on his face. He gives me a nod and a thumbs up. I move into position. Ramaz is ready, and coordinates the opening presentation. Maya Angelou's poem, *Phenomenal Women* rings out loud and clear on the speakers. I have created a slideshow of photographs of my guests, and cries of delight fill the room as they recognise themselves and one another.

The first group of performers are a men's folk choir. Their voices soar up to the Wedgwood blue painted ceiling. They stand resolute and formidable in their nationalism, and the applause that fills the room when they finish is instant and heartfelt. Next, is the turn of Anna, the founder of The Sun Festival. Her wheelchair and dark glasses are soon forgotten by an initially defensive audience as she speaks passionately about her vision for the disabled children of Georgia. Once again, the room is warm with appreciation. Enthusiastic applause follow speaker after speaker, and Natia waits patiently for her chance to speak. Her friends cluster around her, cheering when the Women's Fund highlight how domestic abuse is ignored by the establishment.

During a pause in the speeches, the rhubarb and cream tea accompanies lively conversation. The cakes disappear quickly, and the chinking of cups chimes alongside the air conditioning as it throws out its signature Arctic blast. It is uncomfortably cold, and some people are beginning to complain. I break away from chatting with an ethnomusicologist who has come from Svaneti for the event, and search around the back of the closest AC unit for the off switch. I disconnect all but two of them. To my satisfaction, the hall is noticeably warmer – and quieter – by the time I pick up our conversation where we left off.

Cups perch on laps, and snuggle against chair legs as the second half begins. I notice there are fewer people now. I realise that many of those who have already given their talk have left, taking their entourages with them. Something inside me sinks slightly, but then the voices of the women's choir fill the air in a re-creation of an ancient ritual, and rose petals float across the floor, caught in the eddies created by the remaining switched-on air-conditioning units. I see delight on the face of an actor, who is also one of David's closest friends. Once the applause dies down, voices drop and silence settles. After a moment, I become aware of a shuffling and whispering between members of another women's choir. Natia is due to speak; her place is clearly marked on the programme. I watch as increasingly hostile glances are thrown her way. A wave of cramp pulses through my belly. I reach for the support of a chair as I double over in pain. I turn to see people leaving through the open door, and I catch the chime of a church bell. Suddenly, the spy is there, by my side.

"It will be alright." he whispers.

***

Death Knell

About 45 minutes in, behind
The pleasant clink
Chink of porcelain
Flowers, rhubarb, and cream
Tea, fall-in-love-with-me
Chocolate squares, I hear
The chime of
The death knell.

Tilting slightly, I watch as
My marionette life
Tumbles elegantly, pivots
Re-defined by plot
Scandal
Accusation.

I watch the sky
Fall.

***

The spy helps me into the chair, and my frustration blossoms in my guts at his ministrations. "I'm not an old woman," I snarl at him, slapping his hand away and instantly regretting it. A look of hurt and confusion crosses his face. I sigh. "I'm sorry," I mutter, eyes searching past the backs of people in the crowd for Natia. I had meant to be there, right at the front of the crowd to support her. The wave of pain passes, and I sigh again. I continue to search the crowd. As I glance down at my hands, twisted in my lap, I realise the spy is no longer by my side.

***

Yeah. What she said

Natia got up to speak.

People left
In disgust
Apparently.

Natia finished speaking
There was an exodus
From 73 people, to 36
37 people felt tricked
And were revolted
Apparently.

37 people felt betrayed
And hoodwinked
Apparently.

Now, apparently
(And they mean this as the highest form of insult)
I am a lesbian
Have always been a lesbian
And the whole event was designed
To humiliate them.

Natia said nothing controversial.

She served rich nuggets of wisdom
She shared survival stories to inspire
The people of the world.

***

I was devastated. Tears filled my eyes. More people had left than had stayed. I slumped in my chair, the backs of the other guests a shelter for me to hide behind. I looked up through blurry eyes and saw Natia, surrounded by her friends. Her face was jubilant. She caught my eye, and smiled. Some people had stayed, I reminded myself. I pulled myself up from the chair, and as I walked across the room toward her, the spy pressed some painkillers and a glass of water into my hand.

"Remember what she said." he murmured.

***

What she said

I was there, on May 17th 2013
When 10,000 priests tried to kill me and 49 of my friends.
She said.

I was there May 17th 2013
When the minibus I was bundled into by police officers
Who had, before this point, stood by and watched until it was clear we would be trampled Underfoot
Was rocked, side to side by a priest
With broken teeth
And wild eyes, who beat at the glass until it shattered
And I thought
I am only 24-years-old.

She said
Please look at me
Please see me as a person
See me for me, not for my sexuality.

She said
See, my tears are real
Hear, my sobs, they chime to the same bells
That call you to church each day.

Here, take my hand
Link arms with me
I am warm, I am real
I am me.

She said.
My mother loves me
My father too, my brother loves me
My sister, my sister's children, all love me.

I don't want you to love me, or even like me
I just want you to stop beating me up
Slamming me down
Killing me.

What have I done to you?
Is it my mere existence you hate so much?
Is it because I am a lesbian?
Is it because I am a woman?
Is it because I am not you?

She said
I am Georgian and I am proud
Please see me
Please hear me
I am a proud to be a Georgian woman
I am
Proud.

37 leave
36 stand up to applaud.

***

More tears prick my eyes. I move to be with my friends, who start to sing, and I sing with them. We hold hands. The spy joins the circle from across the room, the Baptists join the circle, the artists make the circle bigger, the professors join the circle. Mravalzhamier fills the circle. My soul soars.

"The whole event was a disaster!" exclaims the journalist who had gate-crashed the event, elbowing her way over to me after the music finally stopped. The spy winks at me from where he helps Ramaz pack away the sound equipment. I take a deep breath, and sink into a chair, motioning for her to join me.

"How so?" I ask.

"She, that lesbian," she spits, still standing, "she was so aggressive, so unnecessary, so loud, so intrusive. She told so many lies." She fixes me with a cold stare. "I am surprised you let her speak." She raises one perfect eyebrow in disdain, and settles herself into the chair opposite me. "You see, Leah," she tells me with confidence, "we do not have homosexuals in Georgia. NGOs say they exist, but we, the people of Georgia," she smirks, giving time for her vile innuendo to sink in, "We do not believe them. What you must understand, Leah," she pats my leg and it takes every ounce of discipline not to flinch away, "is that all this is just a very clever way of getting money out of Europe, by people who like to cause trouble."

I deliberately narrow my eyes as I consider how to respond. "I would prefer to concentrate on what we have achieved here this evening," I tell her, calmly. "More than 100 people chose to come to this event, knowing full well it was potentially contentious," I continue, smiling, holding up my hand to cut off an interruption. "Both speakers and the audience engaged in topics that are taboo in Georgia, and people stayed for as long as they felt they could. Perhaps being able to leave was a novelty to them." I fix her with a patient stare, daring her to interrupt me. After three heartbeats of silence, she looks away. "I understand there is a fear of reprisal in many areas of Georgian life that prevents people from exercising their basic right to express themselves in many ways. Where I am from, what Natia said would be held in high esteem." The journalist fidgeted sulkily like a child waiting to be let out of class. "I think it is a shame that her bravery and integrity is not recognised here." I stand up and hold out my hand. "Thank you for coming," I tell her as she takes my hand limply. "I wish you all the best."

My phone pings as I leave the library: Well done you – exactly right, the first SMS says. More of it, says the second. Your bravery and vision is inspiring, says the third. As I get into the waiting taxi, the phone pings again: Power to your elbow.

21: Goodbye Tbilisi

At last I can go home. The early morning flight means I have not slept. As I pass through passport control, and settle myself with a coffee next to gate 103, I feel an immense wave of relief. This leaving moment has been forever coming and I am glad to wave Eliso goodbye. As I sit, I feel my body starting to relax, despite the undulating and persistent pain from my womb. Scratching my eyes awake, I delve into my rucksack for the box containing Nino's diary. There is one final entry; a single piece of paper, ripped out, folded, and tucked into the back cover. It burns my fingers as I unfold it. A brown water stain has bled beneath the now familiar handwriting.

***

October 20th 1921

Alexei came today to tell Mother that Papa is dead. He had died in a glorious battle, and we should be proud. Mother did not look very proud. She sat down very quickly, and stayed that way for a while, dry-eyed, in the front parlour. Then, she got up and said: "This will not be spoken about again."

Nino

***

The hairs on my arms stand up. I close Nino's diary, slowly. I know I am being watched. Looking up and turning round, I see David. He is just on the other side of the glass. He lifts his right hand, crosses himself, and touches first his lips, and then his heart. I freeze. He turns away, and walks off towards the escalator. Behind him, is a sign, which declares in red: Tbilisi Loves You.

***

Flight home

Ah, the complete
Utter, total
Reliability of the English
Family.

The game of
Travel Scrabble and
That solid certainty
Of the measured, considered
Conversation.

Assailed by pain
I lean forward
Quietly ask if Mother has any
Paracetamol.

I am
Immediately rewarded with
Kind eyes and an innate understanding.
I sip, grateful for the
Spare water donated from her bag.

My exhausted tears spill onto
Scribbled words
Nino's diary sits hot in my hand.

Drifting in and out of their
Conversations, I hear father say
After discussing a dilemma
"Well, my darlings, you must do what you will but
It all depends on
Where your conscience lies."

Acknowledgements

To my son for living with my love-hate, passive-aggressive relationship with Georgia, and still loving me. To Thomas Dunning for understanding what a mess my head has been, whilst trying to figure stuff out. To Aslan for keeping me on the straight and narrow, and asking really hard questions about my motives. To Susan Fothergill, Julie Davis, and Beth Brown for worrying about me but never trying to stop me. For everyone who has heard any of my poetry performed, thank-you for listening. To Eliso Sarava for trying really hard to understand me, travelling with me through Georgia, translating, and making all those delicious cakes. To David Shugliashvili, members of the Sathanao Choir, and Bishop Michael of the Georgian Baptist Church for staying to the end and singing with me. To Natia for being magnificent in the face of adversity. To Nino Kalandadze for travelling with me, sharing her stories and her expertise with me. To Keti Kalandadze for validating and supporting my journey. To Ramaz, who tried, with little understanding of why it hurt so much, to support me. To Jenny Smith, Louise Curtis, and Helen Curtis for listening to me deep into the night, with wine, song, and tears. To William Anderson Gaskill for his insight and skill in the mystical art of the semi-colon. To Ava, my adopted Georgian dog, for absolutely completely believing in me with no judgement and the kindest of hazelnut-brown eyes. To the network of spies, both those I know about and those who you think I don't know about. I could thank you, but then everyone would know who you were. And you would know that I knew who you were. And that would defeat the object.

Endnote:

The Red Army invasion of Georgia (15th February – 17th March 1921), also known as the Soviet-Georgian War, or the Soviet invasion of Georgia, was a military campaign by the Soviet Russian (RSFSR) Red Amy aimed at overthrowing the Social-Democratic (Menshevik) government of the Democratic Republic of Georgia (DRG), and installing a Bolshevik regime in the country. The conflict was a result of expansionist policy by the Soviets, who, until the turbulent events of WWI, aimed to control as much as possible of the lands that had been part of the former Russian Empire. Despite their revolutionary efforts, the mostly Russian-based Georgian Bolsheviks did not have sufficient support in their native country to seize power without external intervention.

The independence of Georgia had been recognized by Soviet Russia in the Treaty of Moscow, signed on 7th May 1920, and the subsequent invasion of the country was not universally agreed upon in Moscow. It was largely engineered by two influential Georgian-born Soviet Russian officials, Joseph Stalin and Sergo Ordzhonikidze, who on 14th February 1921, obtained Lenin's consent to advance into Georgia on the pretext of supporting a 'peasants' and workers' rebellion' in the country. Soviet forces took the Georgian capital Tbilisi, and after heavy fighting, declared the Georgian Soviet Socialist Republic (GSSR) on 25th February 1921. The rest of the country was overrun within three weeks, but it was not until September 1924 that Soviet rule was firmly established. Almost simultaneous occupation of a large portion of southwest Georgia by Turkey (February - March 1921) threatened to develop into a crisis between Moscow and Ankara, leading to significant territorial concessions by the Soviets to the Turkish National Government in the Treaty of Kars.

During the purges by Stalin, when intellectuals, Jews, and Muslims were expelled from Tbilisi, the family of women sent food parcels, every month, to Siberia for four years, encouraged by the Red Army, in the belief that their Grandfather was alive. This much of the story told in Nino's diary is true. The rest of the information is based on research and listening to the stories of those families who survived these years of upheaval. There is some confusion over what exactly happened to Keti's grandfather. However, evidence points to paperwork received by the women on Erekle Street in 1925. It details how an unnamed man, presumably their grandfather, had been shot, his body buried in a mass grave, the very same day he had been taken from the house on Erekle Street back in 1921.